ALSO BY ANNE RENWICK

The Tin Rose

The Golden Spider

The Silver Skull

The Iron Fin

A Trace of Copper

Kraken and Canals

Rust and Steam

IN PURSUIT OF
DRAGONS

An Elemental Web Tale

Anne Renwick

To Huntley,
Here be dragons!
Anne Renwick

www.annerenwick.com

Book Layout ©2015 BookDesignTemplates.com

In Pursuit of Dragons/ Anne Renwick. -- 1st ed.
ISBN 978-1-948359-08-5

Cover design by James T. Egan of Bookfly Design.

Edited by Sandra Sookoo.

To my boys, who love castles, swords and dragons.

THANK YOU TO...

The Plotmonkeys—Kristan Higgins, Shaunee Cole, Jennifer Iszkiewicz, Stacia Bjarnason and Huntley Fitzpatrick—who almost never blink at my bizzare plots and always steer me in the right direction.

Sandra Sookoo, my brilliant editor who mercilessly ferrets out weaknesses and sets my work on a better course.

My husband and my two boys.

My mom and dad.

Mr. Fox and his red pen.

Chapter One

Scotland, March 1885

Natalia Zakharova Kinross, Lady of Kinlarig, knelt on the flagstone hearth seeing to the task of shoveling out the cold, dead ashes of last night's fire. In the far corner of the chamber—part study, part laboratory—a rusty steam maid stood immobile, gathering cobwebs and dust. Coal was too scarce to waste on extravagances such as steambots when one lived in a cold, damp Scottish castle. Particularly when one's husband had preferred to direct all funds to his lavish townhome in Edinburgh.

The rotten, inbred popinjay.

Upon his death, a list of outstanding bills had been forwarded to her. A headache—beginning at the back of her neck and spreading upward to encompass her entire skull—had grown as she'd flipped through sheaves of paper detailing his extensive purchases. Unlike her, her husband—Stuart Kinross, Laird of Kinlarig—had been accustomed to living in luxury. Oolong tea from China. Blood oranges from Spain. Embroidered textiles from India. All indulgences he enjoyed because the Department of Cryptozoology had awarded *her* a generous stipend to conduct research into the therapeutic properties of dragon venom. But the funds were deposited in her husband's accounts, affording him complete and total control; the paltry amount he had allocated to his wife barely covered basic research and household expenses.

Never mind she'd swallowed her pride and begged for more.

Not once in three years had her absent husband deigned to visit his family's ancestral castle, not until the Department of Cryptozoology declined to continue funding her research. With his lifestyle threatened, he'd returned with a sole purpose in mind. Frowning, Natalia sat back on her heels and studied the treasure trove heaped within the fireplace. A dragon that spent her days pillaging the countryside for items he could pawn—golden goblets, strands of lustrous pearls, or gemstone-studded tiaras—might have pleased him. Alas, the dragon collected nothing so grand. Quite simply, he had decided her dragon was worth more dead than alive.

But to knowingly sell his wife's beloved pet to a lowlife like Rathail, a man who would butcher a rare and precious creature, selling the dragon's parts and pieces on the black market to the highest bidder? Comparing her dead husband to a spineless worm was too kind.

A flash of silver caught her eye. That was new. She plucked the coin out of her dragon's treasure trove, leaving Zia's other prized possessions within the fireplace untouched. Scattered throughout a heap of smooth stones fetched from alongside the nearby River Teith were several items of questionable value: silver spoons, shards of a broken mirror, a pewter tankard, twisted fragments of metal, buttons, a pearl earring, a brass shoe buckle, a key, a handful of iron nails. Natalia's dead husband's pocket watch.

A faint—and entirely inappropriate—smile tugged at her lips. She couldn't begrudge Zia her trophy, not after what Kinross tried to do.

Greedy bastard. What had he expected to happen? She shook her head. Trying to cage a dragon with sharp claws and teeth, never mind the poison glands. Served him right for merely pretending to listen when she'd spoken about her research.

Castle Kinlarig was now legally hers, but without funds, continuing to reside within its walls would soon become untenable. But her options were poor. A fugitive from the Russian government, she'd arrived on British shores with nothing to her name save the possession of a very real, mythological creature. Keen to have a dragon on British soil, the Department of Cryptozoology had offered her asylum in the form of a Scottish husband.

Despite the silver threads in his hair, Kinross was no more than a decade or two older than her and still handsome. In the space of a heartbeat, she'd agreed.

Marriage altered her citizenship, provided her a residence outside a quiet, Stirlingshire village, and—via a subsidy—funded her research into the properties of dragon venom.

Still mourning her father, she'd not thought to ask why a Scottish laird would agree to marry a foreign woman, sight unseen. Stupid of her. Her own childhood had been so very lonely that twice now she'd placed her trust in the hands of unworthy men, all in pursuit of safety, security, and hopes of starting a family.

Children, however, were not on Kinross's list of interests. After a perfunctory wedding night, he'd taken his leave, appropriated the vast majority of her money— legally his—and returned to the arms of his mistresses. She'd not seen her husband again. Not until he returned a month past, bringing with him most unwelcome news: he'd sold the dragon. To Rathail, a man who sold exotic animals, piece by piece. Dragon blood. Dragon scales. Teeth. Skin. Bones.

Tucking the coin inside a pocket sewn onto her corset for safekeeping, she bent back to her chore. Her housekeeper, Aileen, would welcome the addition of the half-crown into the household funds. Of late, the cabbage soup they'd been subsisting upon was growing rather thin, a poor substitute for a hot, buttered scone. Her stomach growled. She glanced at the empty bowl resting upon her workbench. They needed money. And the only way to convince the Department of Cryptozoology to renew her grant was to produce results. She was so very close, but how could she continue to collect Zia's venom, depleting her reserves when—

Zia—who had been guarding the door—darted into the great hall. A low, warning hiss skittered over the worn stone floors.

"Come here," a man's voice cajoled, his hands making soft patting sounds. Rathail's hired hunter. A nasty little man who had arrived mere days after Kinross's death, asserting his right to collect one Russian Mountain Dragon. "Come here, girl."

Natalia closed her eyes and muttered under her breath, then leapt to her feet. McKay, her elderly butler, had forgotten again. A lifetime's habit of unlocking the castle's door at dawn was proving impossible to break. It might crush his pride, but she would have to take away his key.

"Do you have a death wish?" she called to Rathail's hunter. She snatched up her crossbow and quiver. "It's unwise to enter without my leave. Again. This behavior is becoming intolerable."

She peered around the edge of the doorframe to the far end of the great hall, marking his position. Tail thrashing, Zia's leathery, vestigial wings unfolded as she rose up onto her hindquarters, unsheathing her claws. Yet still Rathail's man approached, dangling a dead rat by its tail, as if it were a dainty treat when there were hundreds of live rodents in the castle cellars. Teeth bared, Zia lunged, spitting poison. Pungent venom droplets blistered the exposed skin of his hands, and he let loose a string of curses, but the halfwit didn't back away.

Fool.

Saving men from dragons wasn't on her list of tasks for the day, but neither did she wish to have the town judge knocking upon her door. Explaining her husband's gruesome remains had been troublesome enough. Her jaw clenched. The judge had grudgingly accepted her explanation, but a second such death might well land her in prison.

"No good?" Rathail's hunter asked Zia, then threw the rat to the floor in frustration. "Perhaps this will make you more obedient." Crouched low to the ground, he pointed a long metal rod in Zia's direction, backing the dragon into a corner.

Outrage shot through Natalia's nerves. Whatever Rathail's hunter had been paid to collect Zia, he was a stupid man to think any price was worth the risk. But what did she expect? This hunter was a mercenary, motivated by money and unencumbered by ethics. Much like her husband.

Taking a deep, steadying breath, Natalia notched an arrow and began to crank the tension spring. An arrow to his shoulder would send a strong message. The simple cloth of the trousers encasing her legs made no sound as she stepped through the door, braced the crossbow against her shoulder, and took aim.

A second too late.

She fired at the very moment the hunter lunged. *Thwack.* She swore. Her arrow had gone wide, skewering the portrait of an ancient Kinross ancestor instead. Distracted, the man blinked, and Zia lunged, slashing him across the torso, ripping four long gashes through his waistcoat and the shirt beneath. He growled his annoyance from between clenched teeth as blood welled on his chest.

Zia looked up, her golden eyes glinting with pride.

Natalia nodded her approval as she drew another arrow from her quiver, reloading. Rathail's hunter was proving hard to deter. She lifted her weapon. "Go now, and I'll let you live."

Instead of fleeing, the fool looked over his shoulder—a bad plan to break eye contact with a dragon—and unhooked a leather muzzle from his belt. "The creature is bought and paid for, Lady Kinlarig. Rathail is running out of patience. The dragon needs to come with me. Today. Help me crate it, and I'll split the collection fee."

It. He didn't know he was dealing with a female *Laudakia alpino* from the crimson of her dorsal crest scales. Rathail was playing his cards close to his chest, not daring—yet—to send a proper cryptozoologist. Which meant his minion wasn't aware that the venom eating through his skin would keep those claw wounds from healing properly. Another swipe from Zia or an arrow through his chest, and he might well bleed out at her feet.

Natalia spit on the ground. Such an offer wasn't worthy of any other answer.

He narrowed his eyes. "Have it your way."

Without warning the man touched the end of his long, metal rod—a voltaic prod—to Zia's scaly skin. A loud, electric crackle sounded, and Zia jerked, her yellow eyes flashing wide before her knees gave out and she crashed to the floor. With a roar, Natalia pulled the trigger and half a second later her arrow pierced his shoulder.

The man screamed—both in pain and in shock. Had he thought her threat empty?

Her focus narrowed to Zia. Though she was unconscious, her chest rose and fell. The metal rod was intended to stun, not kill. Natalia growled. Not so her crossbow. But she'd missed. Again. Too much time in the laboratory and not enough on target practice.

Enough. Throwing aside her bow and arrows, she drew her blade from its scabbard. Pointing the rapier at him, she ran down the hall with every intention of skewering him to the wall. The man's eyes flashed wide the second before he turned tail and ran.

Natalia dropped to her knee beside the injured dragon, skimming a hand over the charred patch of scales. Zia's slitted eyes opened, and she let out a pitiful mewl.

This needed to end. Instead of following the hunter into the courtyard, Natalia tore up the curving staircase to the castle's curtain wall. Her boots pounded across stone as she ran to a mounted arrow gun. She slid an arrow into its notch and took aim at a waiting clockwork horse. She didn't have to wait long.

Rathail's hunter leapt onto his mechanical beast and threw the lever, but before the contraption could take four steps, Natalia pulled the trigger. *Whoosh!* A second arrow pierced his upper arm. The man screamed as the contraption cantered away down the rough and pitted road. Too far now for her to put an arrow through his neck.

Between his injuries and the venom coursing through his blood vessels, he would need to seek out medical care to survive. In a feverish haze, he might babble about a dragon in a castle. But if the villagers didn't come for her, Rathail's hunter—or another man—would be sent to try again. A knot of worry twisted in her stomach.

She and Zia needed to leave Castle Kinlarig. And soon. But where could they run? All their options were poor. Live rough in the nearby hills of the Trossachs? Without assistance, they wouldn't survive long. Move to her husband's townhome in Edinburgh and sell the castle? A city was no place for a dragon. Flee to yet another country? Zia might end in chains. Or worse.

She couldn't allow the dragon to come to harm. Not after Zia's birth had saved Natalia's life. She rubbed a hand over the back of her neck, across the cluster of dragon scales beneath her scarf. After three years, the evidence of her father's act of treason was still embedded in her very skin. A flash of pain ripped through her. But for the discovery of dragons, she would still be in Russia, still have a father. She might even be married and surrounded by children.

Annoyed at herself for allowing her mind to stray down such pathways, she shook her head and began to lower the weapon. A movement caught her eye. Another man. Walking toward her castle. *Walking!* The audacity!

Had Rathail—tiring of his hunter's inability to complete his assigned task—already sent a new man to collect her dragon?

She notched another arrow.

~~~

Only a handful of sheep dotted the fields on either side of the deserted road that led to Castle Kinlarig. They grazed unaware or unconcerned—impossible to tell with sheep—as a pteryform circled lazily overhead in the dull, gray sky. Late for such a nocturnal creature to still fly, though the sun was noticeably absent. Rumors had reached his ears that the Russians had managed to train—even saddle—a few such creatures. At the unnerving thought, a whisper of worry brushed over his skin, but Luke Dryden saw no rider upon its back.

Unlike the clockwork horse bolting in his direction.

Its rider slumped forward hanging on to the contraption's neck, an arrow—no, two arrows— protruding from his shoulder.

"Turn back!" Eyes wild, the man yanked at the control lever, slowing the horse, but not stopping. His shirt was torn and bloody. Oozing, pitted ulcers spotted the exposed skin of his face and hands. Not a man in any condition to issue orders, yet he tried. "The creature is bought and paid for. The collection contract is mine alone."

"Creature?" Luke hedged, feigning ignorance and nonchalance. But inside his stomach, worry twisted itself into a knot. "Insofar as I am aware, men shoot arrows, not beasts."

No one was supposed to know about Zia. That was the entire reason the Department of Cryptozoology had tucked the dragon away in such a remote location. Hell, he'd even bypassed reporting to his supervisor in Edinburgh—as per protocol—to prevent anyone from following him to this castle, a decision that would likely cost him his job. Yet here was a man ostensibly claiming authority over the Russian Mountain Dragon.

Organic chemistry was Natalia's passion. Fencing followed as a close second, and they'd spent long hours in the great hall, in the castle courtyard, sparing with the antique armor a distant Kinross ancestor had pinned to various walls. A married woman, thus forbidden to him, it was the only physical activity in which they could honorably engage to melt away the tension that stretched between them.

But archery? Not once had he seen her lift the crossbow from the wall, yet—he eyed the man's injuries— her aim was excellent. Still, the dragon's existence was known, and she was taking deadly aim at living men. His stomach twisted. Perseverance and grit had brought him back to Scotland, urging him onward as he traversed mile upon mile. He only hoped he'd arrived in time to extract her from whatever circumstances brought this man to her door.

"A crazy witch defends the dragon," the man spat, his eyes narrow. "Job's barely worth the coin if I have to pay for a suit of armor first." He took in Luke's ragtag appearance, his lack of weaponry, and decided he wasn't competition. "Best turn back, lest she run you through. I'll not be burying your corpse when I return." He shoved the clockwork horse's lever forward and rode away.

Natalia had clearly kept her skills sharp, along with the edge of her blade and the tips of her arrows. For the first time in a short forever, Luke smiled. Hitching his pack higher on his back, he trudged forward, impatient to deliver his news to the woman who held his heart.

He was ten feet from the castle door when an arrow whistled through the air, embedding its tip in the dirt not three inches from his foot. Perhaps his newfound optimism was misplaced. It had been—

"Two years!" Natalia yelled from above.

He glanced up in time to catch a glimpse of her head disappearing behind the parapet.

Shit.

A door at the castle's gate stood open. A pair of rheumy eyes surmounted by white, wiry eyebrows peered at him around its edge, then threw a careful glance over Luke's shoulder. They blinked, and the entirety of old Willie McKay's welcome face appeared.

"Sir." Kinross's ancient butler beckoned him inward. "Your return is fortuitous. Lady Kinlarig is in desperate need of protection. You must take her to Edinburgh immediately and place her under your department's safekeeping." McKay began a slow shuffle down the passageway into the courtyard. "I shall instruct Aileen to pack the lady's trunk."

Flee. Luke agreed with the sentiment, though given that last arrow, she was unlikely to concur. He followed the old man. "Will her husband not object?"

McKay made a most interesting noise in the back of his throat. "The laird passed a month ago."

Hope shot through him. *Not* an acceptable response to such news, but if she was widowed, then she was free to remarry. His stomach sank. Impossible. He wasn't a fit husband for *any* woman. "What happened?"

Clearing his throat, McKay stepped into the courtyard and waved at a large, iron-barred cage that sat atop a steam wagon. "A most unfortunate event—"

Thundering feet sounded. A galloping accompanied by the unmistakable scrape of claws over wood and stone. Forked tongue flicking, Zia half-flew, half-slid down the stairs, scampering across the ground to throw herself against Luke's legs, nearly knocking him to the ground. She looked up at him, her golden eyes shining.

He stroked the smooth scales of her head. "How's my girl doing?" he crooned. Slipping a hand into his pocket, he pulled out a lump of sulfur, both a treat *and* good for a dragon's skin. "Did you miss me?" He held it out on his palm.

Zia nuzzled his hand with her drool-laden lips, swallowing the yellow rock whole, and Luke quickly wiped his hands on his trousers, removing any residual toxin.

A Russian Mountain Dragon, they'd told him at the Department of Cryptozoology three years ago. He'd gaped at them in shock, hardly daring to believe his good luck. By virtue of time served, a number of other employees ranked higher than him, and by rights the assignment should have been theirs. But this undertaking came with a complication that most were unwilling to shoulder. A Russian fugitive married to a notorious, loud-mouthed, skirt-chasing Scottish laird. As tensions between Britain and Russia increased concerning the Afghan border, it was imperative the gentleman be placated and the woman well-settled so her presence in Scotland would not be revealed.

He'd seen to that before he left, extracting promises and assurances from his colleagues that they would monitor her situation while he was away. However, the arrows in the man's shoulder and his words indicated their efforts had been insufficient. Good that he arrived with a plan.

He crouched beside the dragon, frowning as he ran his palm over a charred patch of scales just behind her shoulder. If that man had put this mark upon Zia—

"Luke Dryden." Natalia's voice sliced through the air.

With a final pat to the dragon's head, he straightened and met her ice-blue gaze. *Aether*, he'd missed her. Though, judging from the grip she had on the swept hilt of a sixteenth century Italian rapier, she didn't feel the same. Guilt tightened his chest. He'd been wrong not to say a proper farewell.

Her soft-soled, leather-laced boots didn't make a sound as she descended the stairs into the courtyard, her dark scowl brightened only by golden hair that was swept back from her face, braided and tightly secured in a crowning circlet. About her neck, the ever-present scarf. A corset, cut and boned for ease of movement. Gone were her skirts, replaced by trousers that hugged her lean curves... in a manner that was going to see him killed.

He lifted his gaze and nodded, careful not to smile. "Lady Kinlarig." The moment called for diplomacy. He was, after all, long overdue. "I'm sorry for your loss."

She snorted. "Kinross's death, though unanticipated, was not the least bit objectionable." From the look on her face, his death would also be welcome. "I refuse to mourn."

"Many apologies," Luke began. "I did not intend to be away for so many months."

"Months?" Her eyebrows rose. There was a sharp edge to her voice. "Two *years* have passed without so much as a skeet pigeon. After the actions of your department this past year, or lack thereof, I'm surprised you dare return." She tested the weight of the blade in her hand, as if considering which body part of his to remove first.

Clearly he'd made a mistake, not consulting with his colleagues before returning to Castle Kinlarig. "What—"

She stepped her right foot forward, lifting her blade and widening her stance. "I agreed to marry a degenerate laird on the condition that the Department of Cryptozoology provide me with a yearly stipend. *Me.* Instead, the funds were sent to my thieving husband while I worked tirelessly in the service of the Crown." She pulled a parrying dagger from a sheath on her hip and tossed it at his feet. "It's been months since I last heard from your supervisor. Longer still since any funds were sent."

Tail lashing, Zia backed away, looking from Natalia to Luke, confused. McKay tottered out of range.

Though teaching her to wield a sword had begun in jest, Natalia was a quick study and had soon sought to arm herself against discovery, plucking a variety of different weapons from the castle's largely decorative armory. *Largely.* For—despite its age—this rapier's steel blade gleamed in the dim lamplight. She'd sharpened it. He swallowed. Impossible not to imagine her dragging its long length—over and over—across a whetstone, waiting.

He refused to engage. "I don't want to fight with you," Luke said. "Natalia, we need to *speak.*"

"We will do both." She pointed her chin at the ground. "Pick it up."

A mere courtesy, that dagger. He could not hope to stave off her attack with such a blade. Not for long. And certainly not in his travel-fatigued condition.

She lunged, slicing the tip of her sword through the strap of his pack and dropping it to the ground. "Defend yourself."

With a sigh he picked up the blade. "I can take you and Zia someplace safe."

"I'm not going anywhere with you. Nor is Zia."

She attacked, forcing him to parry with the forte— the thickest part—of his blade. Metal clanged against metal. He rocked into a defensive stance, attempting to throw her blade high using the cross-guard of the dagger's hilt, to execute a croisé. Though the muscles of his arm struggled to execute his brain's demands, he was exhausted and out of practice. She barely stepped backward.

"Pfft. Have you not held a blade in two years?" She advanced, slashing at his stomach, forcing him to leap aside to avoid its tip.

"Not in swordplay." Any knives he'd held had been short, sharp and used with great stealth. Escaping a Russian prison involved no duels of honor.

"Play?" Her eyebrows rose. She attacked again.

He parried and bound down with his dagger, pushing her blade away.

"Better," she snapped, advancing upon him with increased speed. Blades clanged and scraped against each other as they circled about the courtyard. She was toying with him, else she'd have already drawn blood. If this was what she needed to release her anger so they could speak rationally, he would oblige.

But his heavy, thick-soled boots weren't made for agility. They were better suited to hiking through mountains. His heel caught upon the edge of a stone, and he tripped. As his arse landed on hard-packed dirt, his dagger slipped, and the tip of Natalia's rapier sliced through the skin of his forearm. He hissed in pain.

No sympathy was forthcoming. Instead, the sole of her shoe planted itself in the middle of his chest, forcing him to lie flat upon the ground. Lips pressed into a flat line, she leaned over his sprawled form, both triumphant and disgusted. "Never have you been so weak, moving like a slug."

Insults. But such a relief to finally hear her voice again. He grunted. "It's been a rough few years."

Confusion twisted her face, and she bent closer. "Why are your eyes yellow?"

CHAPTER TWO

Withdrawing her foot from Luke's chest, Natalia held out her hand. They clasped forearms, and she hauled him to his feet. Already the blood dried upon his other arm; her cut merely superficial. Though she was barely breathing deeply, his breaths came fast and shallow. Only now, with most of her irritation burned away, did she see the hollows beneath his cheekbones. His lean, spare frame. His pale skin. Lines bracketed his eyes and mouth, ones that shouldn't be there. If one were to judge solely from his face, ten years had passed, not two.

But most telling, the whites of his eyes were so yellow they fairly glowed. One needn't be a physician to recognize the many features of chronic hepatitis, rapidly progressing to cirrhosis. A chill ran over her. What had happened to him while he was away?

Still, an apology refused to pass her lips. Was it too much to ask for a brief note explaining his return was delayed due to illness? She thought of him as a friend. More than a friend, if she were being honest with herself.

"McKay," she began. "Ensure the front door and the gate are securely locked before resuming your vigil. No one is expected until William's lesson this afternoon."

McKay brightened at the prospect of the young man's arrival. "I've some crates for him to shift in the cellars, afterwards. Those Venetian goblets are packed away down there somewhere. They should fetch a few pounds." He shuffled back to the castle's gate.

Luke's calloused hand slipped free of hers and, as his arm fell away, she turned a stiff back upon him and mounted the stairs that led into the foyer while sliding her rapier into its sheath. Zia flutter-hopped up the stairs in front of her, disappearing into the castle. He followed.

"William?" he asked.

"A student," Natalia answered. "To keep my blade skills well-honed, I took on a boy I caught sneaking about the castle's grounds." Without a partner, her opponents had been limited to immobile steambots and bales of hay. She waited for him to object, to lecture her as to the faulty wisdom of her decision. He was, after all, the one who had taught her much about swordplay. A touch of heat rose to her cheeks.

Soon after her disappointing wedding, Luke had arrived at Castle Kinlarig, tasked with composing a lengthy report detailing the requirements for establishing a dragon refuge in Scotland. Alas, a dragon confined to a castle did precious little, save shift in tiny increments to follow a rectangular box of sunlight as it moved across the floor.

Bored, he'd dogged her steps, watching her in the laboratory as she painstakingly studied dragon venom— carefully suctioning a few microliters at a time from Zia's poison glands—in an attempt to analyze its many protein components.

Isolating the individual peptides, she hoped to determine which were responsible for the massive drops in blood pressure and increased bleeding in the dragon's victims. The difference between poison and pharmaceutical was often a matter of dose. Potential applications included a treatment for elevated blood pressure and congestive heart failure.

But research was categorized by bursts of activity followed by long periods of *in*activity. And instead of paying attention to her notes, she'd fallen into deep conversations with Luke... and in love with the wrong man.

She'd needed a distraction, something to diffuse the heat building between them. Teasing him about how the Department of Cryptozoology required its employees to pass a basic qualification test in sword skills, she had pried a rapier off the wall of the great hall and begun wildly swinging it about.

Laughing, he'd quickly disarmed her, then offered lessons. She'd accepted. Day after day, hour after hour, he ran her through a variety of exercises—attack and parry, advance and retreat—until her legs threatened to buckle beneath her. All their physical frustration channeled into intense training sessions—swords clanging as Aileen frowned with disapproval—still hadn't defused desires. Particularly as her skills began to match his.

Impossible not to recall the approval upon his lips, the slow brush of his gaze as it fell to her waist, her hips, tracing the outline of her curves the day she'd first presented herself wearing loose trousers. With the twisting, tripping folds of her skirts eliminated, she'd soon discovered a new talent... and won her first bout.

"Natalia." Beneath the dark shadow of the entryway, Luke caught her arm. She turned, the words on the tip of her tongue dying as she stared into his brown eyes. "I've much to tell you. Contacting you was impossible, but know you were always on my mind." He stepped closer, brushing his knuckles over her cheek. "I can't tell you how many times my mind replayed our last moment together."

When he'd stolen a forbidden, yet chaste, kiss. Time fell away. Her heart began to pound. Anger ebbed as she considered apologizing for her hasty judgment. But it had been years. Could she still trust him?

All those ours they'd spent together, talking. She *knew* him. Knew that as a child he'd purchased a hyena fish from a traveling salesman, that he'd snuck into a circus tent to beg a ride on the back of a camel, that London's kraken infestation had inspired him to study cryptozoology. In turn, she'd told him what it was like to grow up in Russia without a mother and within a community of scientists who single-mindedly served the nearby research facility, a village where textbooks were prized and novels were scorned. No one knew her better.

Now he was back and, though her mind counseled restraint, her heart begged for a chance. She angled her face upward. "I'm free now."

"So you are," he whispered, offering a weak smile. "I'm sorry for any difficulties you face due to his death, but I'm not at all sorry to find you widowed. And despite your welcome at the point of a sword, I'm beginning to believe you missed me."

Zia scampered in circles about their feet, her hide banging against Natalia's leg and throwing her off balance. She stumbled closer to Luke. She should admit nothing, keep her thoughts close. But she wanted him to know how deeply his desertion had hurt her.

"Dreadfully," she confessed. "With every fiber of my being. Every day, every hour, every minute. You went to Russia, didn't you?"

"I—" He clearly thought better of making excuses. "Yes. How could I not?"

"Even though I warned you not to go. Even though you didn't do me the simple courtesy of telling me you intended to go despite my wishes." She jabbed a finger into his chest. "When your absence passed its sixth month, when winter swept into Russia, I was certain you'd either been burnt to a crisp by dragon's breath, or frozen inside a snowdrift."

"I never stopped thinking of you." Hunger flared in his eyes. "And I'm very much alive."

"Are you?" She closed her eyes and lifted her chin, a clear invitation. "Prove it."

His mouth descended upon hers. Soft, warm, and oh so welcome. His kiss was tentative at first, as if he expected she might push him away. And well she ought.

Instead, she grabbed his shirt and yanked him against her chest, releasing all the suppressed attraction that had crackled and flashed between them long ago. His visits to study Zia, to record details about a dragon's biology and behavior, had been the highlight of her time in Scotland. And a miserable torment of aching desire. Finally, they were both free to fan that spark.

He dropped his bag and caught her face in his rough hands, deepening their kiss. She welcomed the invasion of his tongue as proof that their desire for each other had not dimmed. If anything, it had grown more desperate with each passing day. He tore his lips away, and they stared at each other, both uncertain.

"Lady Kinlarig." Aileen's strident voice flung them apart. Only four years separated them in age, but McKay's granddaughter had taken an instant dislike to Natalia, a foreigner of no consequence married to the laird without warning or ceremony. Any number of village girls had turned up their noses at Natalia for having swept away their dreams of becoming lady of the castle.

Heat flooded Natalia's cheeks, not from shame, but from allowing her housekeeper to discover her locked in Luke's embrace in what ought to have been a private moment. She forced out the first polite words that rose to mind. "Mr. Dryden has made an unexpected return."

"I see." In her hands, Aileen held a tray. Every morning, she delivered a simple repast to the high table that stretched across the dais at the far end of the great hall, for she refused to enter the laboratory. Once, the task had fallen to the multitude of steambots Kinross had purchased, before household finances became strained and he abandoned the idea of modernizing the castle. Coal was too dear to waste on such luxuries now. Instead, the metal servants now stood to the side of the great hall in a row, blending in with the occasional suit of armor. Though a chill always hung in the vast room, eating in a laboratory was always ill-advised.

"Welcome back, Mr. Dryden." Aileen's face was pinched as she gave the dragon a wide berth. She detested Zia and was happiest when the creature remained inside Natalia's laboratory. "Would you care for some breakfast? It's rather simple, I'm afraid, given our circumstances."

Hoisting his bag, Luke trailed behind the lure of hot tea and cabbage soup, engaging Aileen in chatter. Natalia hung back, lifting fingertips to her lips.

At last. She was free to pursue Luke, to lure him to her bed. A smiled curved her lips upward. From his passionate kiss, she suspected only a minimum of effort would be needed. His attentions—she was certain of it— would not be a disappointment. Though there was the not-so-insignificant question of what ailed him. And the possibility he would recoil at the sight of her bare neck.

Her smile fell away as she recalled her wedding night. After a simple ceremony here in the great hall, Kinross had swept her off her feet, carrying her up the curving stairs to toss her upon a mattress.

His enthusiasm had raised her hopes. After all, a gentleman who had spent the better part of his life in the city surrounded by elegant ladies ought to know his way around female anatomy. Alas, his focus was less upon her as a woman and more upon consummating the marriage with all due speed. After the initial shock, she'd warmed to the act only to be abandoned upon his bed before she could reach—

She frowned.

"Wedded and bedded," her new husband had declared, mere minutes later as he rolled from the mattress. He'd buckled his trousers, bidding her to readjust her clothing, to button her bodice to her chin, to wrap her scarf about her neck. "Hide those beastly scales, and keep them hidden, lest you wish the villagers to turn on you." He'd thrown a punch card upon the bedside table. "I'm off. If this time didn't take, we'll worry about heirs once you've adjusted. Maintain the old family pile of stones as best you can. Send a skeet pigeon if you must."

By the time she'd reached the window, Kinross's steam carriage was rattling down the road. It was the last she'd seen of her husband.

Until he returned for her dragon.

At her feet, Zia let out a soft whimper.

She strode across the hall. That horrid man's past actions continued to plague her. The best she could say about Kinross was that he hadn't mentioned the scattering of dragon scales at the base of her neck to a single soul. A dragon was a fascinating creature, one any number of men would pay dearly to possess. Should her own secret be discovered, she herself might end up under the microscope. Had her dragon not dispatched her husband, would he have sold his wife as well?

Zia dashed across the great hall to Luke's side.

"A year of mourning is traditional," Aileen muttered as she passed Natalia on her way back to the kitchen.

"Yet I must take actions now," Natalia snapped, dropping the silver coin from Zia's treasure hoard upon the empty tray. "Without coin, food and coal cannot be purchased. Eventually, we will run out of luxuries to barter. I intend to depart for Edinburgh soon." Perhaps Luke could argue her case before the director of the Department of Cryptozoology. She would ask. What other choice was left to her? "If you and your grandfather do not wish to accompany me, perhaps your fiancé ought to have the banns called?"

"Perhaps." Aileen agreed, but she bit her lip. Had the romance gone sour? "I'll speak with him." Her leather soles struck the flagstone with more force than necessary as she exited.

Natalia had not yet met this mysterious fiancé. Nor had Aileen offered to introduce them. She suspected she would not be invited to attend the wedding.

She sat beside Luke at the high table, and he pushed a cup of steaming tea in her direction, all while rubbing

Zia's head. The dragon sat, leaning against a friend she must have thought long lost. "Thank you." Cradling the warm teacup in her hands and watching him drain his bowl of the much-detested cabbage soup, she cut to the quick. "You're ill."

"A filterable virus." A shadow crept across his face. "Forcibly acquired while in captivity at a secret Russian biotechnology laboratory—Ural Zavód—in the Ural Mountains. They were in need of infected human subjects upon which they might trial an experimental medication. It failed. All subsequent formulations also failed to effect a cure. Long-term ramifications persist." He tugged a paper packet from his pocket and poured a brown, powdered substance—an herb—into his teacup. "Milk thistle," he offered by way of explanation. "An attempt to alleviate some of the damage done to my liver." An earthy scent wafted up as he poured his tea over the ground seeds.

"Ural Zavód," she repeated as her mind spun back the clock. Papa had worked there and, when her aptitude for chemistry became apparent, she too had been recruited. She'd even thought to marry a colleague, though she counted herself lucky to have escaped the callous, malevolent man's grasp. Was it Dimitri who had experimented upon Luke, who had tortured him in the name of science? She couldn't bring herself to ask. But it certainly explained why he'd been unable to contact her. A weight in her chest lifted, even as her stomach twisted at the thought of what Luke must have endured.

"I warned you against the attempt. Collecting dragon eggs was a dangerous endeavor, even before scientists—accompanied by armed guards—began to actively hunt them."

"We've had this argument." He met her gaze with a set jaw, unapologetic. "Zia—to my knowledge—is the sole female dragon on the British Isles. Her kind is rare, even in the Urals. Given how prized they are, well, without a male, the species might well face extinction."

Luke shared her father's dream, to establish a refuge in the hills of Scotland where the dragons might live free. He'd fought for the right to launch an expedition into the Ural Mountains of Russia for an entire year. But the Department of Cryptozoology cited increasing tensions with Russia. Expedition denied.

Still, he'd gone. *Insane, driven man.*

"Yet you return empty-handed." Both men had risked so much for so little. One had lost his life; one had lost his health. At least Luke wasn't here to take Zia from her. She pressed a palm to the surface of the worn, wooden trestle table as a new fear raised its head. "Were you followed?"

"Not to my knowledge."

Wonderful. Yet another worry took its place in the queue, clamoring for attention. As if the trouble Lord Kinross had drawn down upon her wasn't enough. If this kept up, she would soon run out of arrows. Or be forced to start aiming for men's throats. An unsettling possibility. She cursed under her breath.

The Department of Cryptozoology's failure to provide a stipend this past year was the root cause of her current predicament. Not, it appeared, that Luke was to blame. He'd been abroad, imprisoned, suffering horrific torment. They would need to speak of that. Soon. Not just yet, but where to start?

"But it appears trouble preceded me." Brow furrowed, Luke placed his hand over hers. "The cage in the courtyard, has it anything to do with the laird's death? With the injured man I met claiming rights to seize a dragon?"

"Everything." Her mind flashed back to her husband's last words.

"We've a meeting," he'd informed her. "With a man who will solve our financial woes and remove the creature to his care."

"What!" she'd cried. "How dare you? Zia is mine!" Inasmuch as one could *own* a Russian Mountain Dragon.

"No," he'd replied with entirely too much calm. "We married *before* the most recent Married Women's Property Act was passed. All you possess—livestock included—belongs to me."

Livestock!

All her moveable property had become her husband's upon the consummation of their marriage. Never had she been so grateful she'd kept her father's research notes a secret. Yet, with Kinross's death, everything that was his—including this castle—was now hers.

Save the one thing she held most dear.

Luke squeezed her hand, dragging her back to the present. "Natalia?"

She blinked. Focused on his worried expression. "Zia ate him."

His jaw dropped.

"Most of him." Natalia swallowed. It had been a horrible, horrible moment. Not at all an end she would have wished upon anyone. Yet once Kinross had enraged the dragon, instinct had overcome training, and the beast inside Zia ripped free... and into the man who would see her caged, quartered, and sold in pieces for profit.

She pulled her hand away, dropping it to stroke the scales upon Zia's head. The dragon sat between their chairs, eyes closed, her small wings folded tightly against her back, thrilled that her two most favorite people were once again in the same room. Natalia elaborated. "She's but a small dragon, unable to eat a full-grown man in one meal. Enough remained that the village doctor was able to conclusively identify him."

"Zia ate him," he repeated, still gaping.

"I'm to blame for the current hysteria surrounding the rumor of a man-eating pteryform." Natalia glanced down. "A mistake. Some of the locals are terrified. Others are mounting expeditions to bring down the creature. I'm not proud of the misdirection, but pointing out that there's been a dragon in their midst for three years seemed unwise."

Luke barked a laugh. "I see." He stabbed his fingers into his hair and dragged his hand to the back of his neck. "I'm struggling with the concept of Zia attacking someone. She's always been a gentle dragon. She never showed any aversion for Kinross before." He closed his eyes briefly. "The cage. He tried to force her inside?"

She nodded. "Exactly. He sold her, as livestock, for an impressive sum to a man named Rathail. But Zia is no farm animal; she is a rare and protected species. I instructed my husband's solicitor to return the funds, but he claims the money was used to address the deep debt Kinross had accrued, and Rathail continues to insist the dragon is his rightful property."

CHAPTER THREE

"Rathail," Luke repeated.

Shit. Shit. Shit.

After all the pains he'd taken to elude the Russians as he exited their frigid wasteland of a country, Rathail's involvement had already exposed Zia to those unscrupulous men who specialized in selling the parts and pieces of rare and emerging animals. Kraken claws. Pteryform wings. Dragon's blood.

Not that the man or his clients would stop at blood. A vial of poison milked from Zia's jaw would sell for thousands. She also possessed wings, claws, teeth and scales. And those were merely surface features. It pained him to consider what a dragon's liver might be worth on the black market.

"You know him?" Her eyes narrowed.

"Of him." Had Luke or any of his colleagues met him, the man would be behind bars. But the name "Rathail" was an alias. "An unscrupulous trader of exotic animals, he has a price on his head."

"How much?" A mercenary light ignited in her eyes.

"Absolutely not." He shook his head vehemently. A mistake. He hadn't had a decent night's rest in... years. Their earlier skirmish had awakened the dull headache that had plagued him for months. "Are the castle's finances so awful?"

"Worse." She stood, crossing her arms and frowning. "Hence my husband's attempts to sell Zia. I own a castle and a townhome in Edinburgh and have no funds with which to maintain them. I've sold what I can, exchanging candlesticks and crystal for coal and food. But the villagers haven't much coin, and what use do they have for dark and dingy portraits of Kinross ancestors?" She waved her hand at the great hall.

His eyes caught upon one in particular. An arrow pierced its canvas, protruding from the chest of a dignified and bewigged gentleman. But she was correct. Two long, wooden tables and their chairs stretched the length of the room, their surfaces bare. The mantle too lacked adornment. Gone were any and all decorative ornaments.

He smiled at the mental image of Natalia arriving in the small, Scottish village with a sword strapped to her hip and her arms full of antiques, bartering them away for tea and biscuits.

"It's not funny," she huffed. "Kinross was never generous with funds. But now I've not a farthing left to pay Aileen or McKay. Zia is subsisting on the occasional sheep and whatever fish she manages to catch in the river." She began to pace. "I contacted the Department of Cryptozoology regarding my situation and was sent nothing but a note conveying 'their deepest condolences'. Without results, they've no interest in funding me or my research. I intend to take up residence in the Edinburgh townhome. From there I'll either need to sell the castle or remarry."

He frowned at the thought of Natalia remarrying. He selfishly wanted her for himself, but he had precious little to offer her beyond helping to extract her from this current situation. "Rathail will not cease his attempts to capture Zia, not even if you kill this current hunter. Appealing to the legal department to contest Rathail's claims will do no good. The man is a ghost. Besides, if my department has ceased to provide funds..." During his absence someone had badly mishandled her case.

"Exactly." She threw her hands in the air. "Traveling to the city, however, is proving an impossibility. The steam wagon is broken, Zia is deeply averse to being caged and, even were we to manage all that, setting out upon the road makes us an easy target for Rathail's hunter. To say nothing of managing a dragon in a city."

"All true. Regardless, neither of you are safe here. Zia will not fare well in a smaller home. She needs more space, not less." At the sound of her name, the dragon shifted her weight, nudging his leg in a clear ploy for attention. He swallowed the rest of his tea—its bitter, weedy taste a necessary evil to assist his damaged liver's functions—then obliged Zia. "Best to evacuate the premises quickly while the hunter is recovering."

"And where, pray tell, would you have us go? Into the highland moors?" She narrowed her eyes. "That's exactly what you have planned. *What* are you not telling me?"

It was time. He hoped she wouldn't skewer him. "Upon docking in Edinburgh, I didn't report in to my department. Nor did I come directly here. My brother met me before I even stepped from the ship."

"He's still the gamekeeper for Castle Edinample?"

"He is. A qualified—if unpracticed—assistant. My two years in the Ural Mountains of Russia were not wasted. I did not come home emptyhanded." A grin stretched his face. "I passed him a very important bundle. A male dragonet. My brother waits for us in the Trossachs."

"How?" Natalia gasped, her eyes wide and dancing.

Luke sat a bit taller in his chair as his chest swelled with pride. He had, after all, accomplished the near impossible. "The facility was compromised. Something about the capture and interrogation of a Russian agent in Germany. Equipment and research subjects—prisoners— were being transported to a new location. Mistakes were made, doors were left unlocked. In the chaos, a few other men and I took advantage to break free." No need to tell her about the man he'd killed for the clothes on his back, the keys at his hip. "There was a new dragonet in a cage—a month or two old—I took him with me." Along with a few other items he'd pawned in Riga. "I managed to gather enough rubles to buy a steamer ticket and send a single skeet pigeon."

"Not to me," she huffed.

"No. Absolutely not. The dragon's trail needed to go cold, in case…" His smile faltered. "In case my path had been traced. The timing of the dragon's escape linked to mine. Or my connection to you somehow discovered." He looked away. "During the acute stage of hepatitis, during their horrible 'treatments', I was often delirious with fever. I can't be certain what—if anything—I revealed."

She took his hand, her eyes conciliatory. "You made the right choice, passing the dragonet to him. Not that I'm happy you ignored my warnings. Or didn't tell me about your expedition before you left."

"I thought I'd be gone a few months at most," he confessed. Zia nudged his hand with her snout, insisting he resume his attentions.

"What did you name him, the dragonet?"

"Sasha, after your father."

"He'd have liked that." She blinked back the tears that welled in her blue eyes. "A companion for Zia at last, even if he is merely a dragonet."

Luke stood, gathered Natalia against his chest and kissed the top of her head. When she'd run from Russia, two dragonets had been under her care. Yuri, a young male dragonet, hadn't survived the journey.

Though he offered sympathy, it was impossible to ignore the sweet scent of her soap or the soft warmth of her curves. When she melted against him and her arms wrapped about his waist, his mind strayed to their earlier, interrupted kiss. He let his hand drift up her spine to cup the base of her skull. A widow, she was no longer forbidden. His honor and her virtue would not suffer if—

At his feet, Zia nudged his leg again, harder. Enough to upset his balance. There would be no ignoring her. "What is it, girl?"

The dragon stared at him for a moment with unblinking golden eyes, then turned and left the room. Flapping her wings, she half-flew, half-hopped though the door leading into the adjacent room. Once styled the Earl's Presence Chamber—a title long-since extinct— the room now served as Natalia's laboratory, and its fireplace held Zia's treasure trove.

Zia's head appeared in the doorway to see if they followed.

With a sigh, Natalia released him. "If we're to leave, I've a single request." Her face flushed pink, and his heart ceased to beat while he waited for her next words, hoping. "Share my bed tonight?"

He stopped breathing. "You're certain?" He'd hardly dared hope for her forgiveness, let alone such an invitation. His groin stirred. If only he could sweep her off her feet, he would carry her to her bedchamber this very second. "I'm not at my best." And never would be again. But if she still wanted him…

"Was our earlier kiss not demonstration enough? I'm tired of regrets, and we've waited long enough. Don't make me ask again." Even her ears were now red.

"Oh, I won't." He tucked a stand of golden hair behind her ear, then leaned close to whisper, "The moment I first laid eyes on you, I was lost." She shivered as he pressed his lips to the edge of her jaw, working his way back to her sweet lips. "And there's no need to wait for nightfall."

Zia hissed her impatience, and Natalia sighed. "The interruptions won't cease until we see what Zia is about." Her palm ran over the rough surface of his beard, and a teasing light flickered in her eyes. "But then..."

It took every last effort to step away from her, but the sooner Zia was allowed to show him her latest treasure, the sooner she would settle.

Luke scanned the room as he entered. Alongside one wall stretched a length of tables and cabinets placed end-to-end, their surfaces covered with all manner of chemistry equipment. Beakers and burets. Crucibles and clamps. Filters and flasks. The same cluttered chaos he recalled.

Only now weapons were everywhere. A staggering array of sharp, steel edges gleamed. Propped against the wall, hung from hooks, piled in corners were swords, crossbows, bows and arrows. Even a pike. "It's a wonder there are any weapons left in the great hall."

"We found more stored in the cellars." She lifted a shoulder. "I can't spend every hour at the workbench." She picked up a crossbow and slid a palm over the wooden surface of its tiller as he hoped she might soon run her hand over his— "Swordplay, target practice, knife throwing, all diversions that have proved useful. Save the rifles. I've not the powder or the bullets."

Thank aether.

Clamping his jaw shut and ignoring the curved stairs in the corner that led to her bedchamber above, he turned his attention to Zia, kneeling beside her on the thick carpet that stretched before the hearth. The dragon was shoving aside rocks, bits of metal and such, hunting for a particular item she wished to display. He waited patiently.

No fire burned in its grate, but hearth tools lay scattered upon the ground. "You were interrupted."

"By that scoundrel who bore away two perfectly good arrows." She frowned and shifted on her feet. "Ever since... since Zia ate Kinross, she's almost refused to leave her fireside treasures. It's been a cold winter. I've been rationing coal, but—" Natalia gasped and clamped a hand over her mouth.

Zia stepped backward, raising up on her forelegs to lift her gaze to them both. Pride rippled over her reptilian features. Protruding from her pile of treasures were five eggs. Five *dragon* eggs. Light brown, each had red-gold streaks branching across its surface, streaks of lightning that glinted in the faint light.

Speechless, Luke ripped his gaze away from her clutch to stare at the proud mother. His expedition into the Urals had been aimed at this very outcome, yet she'd managed to handle this all on her own.

The dragon nudged his hand, pushing it toward her nest.

Permission granted, Luke reached out and scooped a leathery egg from the hoard with both hands. The smooth egg was warm to the touch.

"Impossible!" Natalia cried, pressing a hand to her heart. "Isn't it?"

Zia flicked her tongue and tipped her head. As he stared—stunned—the dragon opened her mouth and—very carefully—retrieved the egg from his hands. She deposited it back atop her treasure alongside the other eggs, then buried them once again beneath the stones. Once more the dragon nudged at his hands, pushing them toward a pile of cold ashes, urging him to light a fire beside her nest.

"Nest," he said aloud, finding his voice at last. Smiling, he caught Natalia's wide-eyed gaze. "It's not a treasure hoard, it's a nest. And she wants us to keep the fire burning to incubate her eggs. Without the fire, there's no chance the eggs will hatch." In their natural habitat, a male—usually of a mated pair—would spit fire upon the rocks, heating them. But therein lay the problem. Only a *male* Russian Mountain Dragon could breathe fire. As his quest had failed, Zia had no choice but to turn to humans for help. Excitement rippled over him. They needed to shoulder the responsibility of keeping the stones warm.

He shoveled away the cinders and lifted the coal scuttle. Barely any lumps lay within. He set them all upon the grate. "We'll need more coal. Or peat. Anything that will burn." Hell, he'd reduce the castle's furniture to sticks if necessary. If these eggs were viable, it was nothing short of a miracle.

CHAPTER FOUR

"But... how?" Natalia handed Luke a box of matches. There was precious little coal remaining in the household. Sufficient to last a few more weeks if they were careful. "How could she have produced eggs without the male of her species?"

"Parthenogenesis." The excitement of discovery filled his voice. His eyes sparkled and gleamed.

A shower of sparks fell upon the coal. One caught, and Luke gently blew the tiny flame to life, momentarily distracting her with the sight of his well-formed posterior. How many times had she admired it in times past? Was it as firm as it looked? Blue flames of lust blazed across her skin. She'd know soon enough. He sank back onto his heels, and the flames licking at the coal threw a flickering light across the planes and angles of his face where his experiences these past years had carved the features of his face into hard relief. Dark eyebrows slashed across his face in deep concentration, and there was a slight crookedness to the bridge of his nose as if it had been broken. A faint, white scar cut through the lower edge of his lip. How was it possible he was yet more breathtakingly handsome?

"Parthenogenesis," she repeated, forcing her mind to focus on the miracle before them.

The odd term stirred a distant and faint memory. With precious little known about the natural history of dragons, her father had been nothing short of obsessed by the reproductive biology of monitor lizards, thought to be the dragon's closest living relative. Speculation often turned to reproductive behavior.

"Virgin birth," she said softly. How her father would have loved to witness this moment. "A hotly-debated topic among herpetologists, if I recall correctly." She stared down at the pile of metal and stone covering Zia's eggs. All this time she'd been oblivious of their presence. She frowned. Why hadn't Zia tried to alert her? Only now, with the arrival of her favorite, indulgent human did she proudly display her clutch. Had Zia assumed Natalia already knew, given her human had tirelessly stoked the dragon's fire these past six weeks?

"Exactly." Luke's eyes danced. "It's an extremely rare event. An egg formed without fertilization by the male of the species. First observed by Charles Bonnet in 1740. A reproductive strategy mostly confined to invertebrates but known to occur upon rare occasions in amphibians and reptiles."

Luke's exhilaration failed to ignite her own. She was happy for Zia, of course, but this complicated everything immeasurably. Yet another variable, yet another worry to weigh upon her mind. One dragon in Edinburgh would be difficult, but a dragon with five dragonets? She shook her head.

Zia, whose gaze had not left the growing fire, let out a heavy sigh and lowered herself onto the hearthrug. A moment of peace, though the charred mark upon her scales was a stark reminder of the dangers they faced. The eggs must remain a secret. Aether forbid Rathail or his hunter learned of them. Their value on the open market would be incalculable. Attacks to secure Zia and her clutch would be relentless. Natalia could deter the occasional hunter, but holding her ground in an all-out siege upon the castle was another thing altogether. Her chest tightened at the memory of Yuri's tiny body tucked inside her coat, of the scratch of his claws on the skin of her throat, of his eyes closing never to open again. The cold and wet of the Baltic Sea had been too much for the tiny dragonet. Traveling into the hills and mountains of the Trossachs... There was no choice but to delay their travel plans.

"How long must the eggs incubate?" she asked, wrapping her arms across her chest. The presence of these eggs ought to bring her joy. Instead, memories kept knocking at a door she'd locked shut long ago.

"No one is certain," he said. "A seven to eight-week incubation is the estimate recorded in the archives by Sir

Ridley Sutton, but he was only recording mythology and hearsay, not fact."

"Zia started begging for fires six weeks past." Shortly after eating Kinross. Aether, she hoped human consumption wasn't a prerequisite for dragon reproduction. "If that's when she laid the eggs, they'll require heat for another week. Possibly two." Her voice was clipped. "I don't suppose he made mention of an exact temperature?"

Luke snorted. "No. But given the males spit fire to heat the rocks, we can conclude it's well above human body temperature."

That fit with her recollection of the dragon egg hunt. The soldiers had tended fires in anticipation of a find while she and the others scaled the rocky cliffs, searching for dragon eggs. She spun away and began to pace, rubbing the scales at the back of her neck beneath her scarf. A successful hunt, but one that had ended tragically for her when she'd slipped and fallen. "We can't leave. Not until they've hatched."

"I disagree." His voice was hard, determined. "Staying here is not an option. This complicates our preparations—we'll need a brazier—but it does not render travel unfeasible." Luke frowned, his tone softening. "Natalia, what is it? What aren't you telling me?"

Secrets from her past boiled to the surface. Nothing she wasn't prepared to share with him, after all, intimacy would lay them bare. Forcing the words from her lips, however, was proving difficult. She'd never divulged her memories of her accident, of those days she'd clung tenuously to life, not with anyone. Like a spark landing upon dry tinder, emotions threatened to overcome her. One moment she'd clung to those rocks with stands of her hair whipping about her face, tossing a smile at Dimitri as they neared the cave's edge. The next moment, all her plans, all her love and hope for the future had been dashed upon the sharp rocks below.

"Natalia?" Luke's voice called as if from far away.

But from that pit of despair, hope had emerged. Her father had saved her, restored her ability to walk. She glanced at her workbench. She had Papa's notebook, a collection of scientific equipment and reagents. Certainly she was no cell biologist, but she could follow a protocol. Luke might live for years, but his health would steadily decline. It already had. Gone was the robust vitality she remembered, though the grit and determination she'd always admired still blazed. She wanted him.

But these dragon eggs presented her—him—with a unique opportunity. One she'd never spoken of. A possibility that hadn't existed in over three years. Her husband, the blackguard, had glimpsed the results of her secret and recoiled. Would Luke? No. But neither did she wish to be placed under the microscope. Yet she could not withhold the possibility of a cure. How—where—to begin?

She forced her feet to stop, her fingers to unlatch from her arms, and lifted her gaze to his questioning eyes. She needed to tell him everything. He deserved to know. "When the eggs hatch, I might be able to..."

"We can't stay here, waiting for the dragonets to hatch. Easier to transport them now." Luke unbent from his position on the floor and stood. He swayed and caught himself on the mantle as all the blood drained at once from his face.

She rushed to his side, offering a steadying hand. "What's wrong?" She regretted their earlier skirmish. He was too drained.

"I'm fine," he insisted.

"You're not." Even Zia looked up in alarm. Did he not trust her enough to let down his own guard?

His shoulders sagged in admission. "My condition flares from time to time, when I'm ill or overtired. I might have pushed myself a bit too hard during that last leg of my journey home."

Home. To her, not his family. Her heart squeezed. "It's more than that," she said.

This wasn't something rest could cure. The ultimate outcome of his captivity in Russia would be a prolonged and painful death. She refused to dismiss his condition. He *needed* more than milk thistle tea. "Did they treat you with dragon's blood?"

She'd asked Papa about such treatments once, the day he'd pressed her to develop a sulfated purine derivative in her laboratory, an immune-suppressing drug he hoped might enable him to transplant dragon tissues into humans. Even then, she'd questioned the wisdom of such experiments. Glancing at Zia, bedded down before the fire, she recalled his words.

"*Da.* Dragon's blood treats. It does not cure. Not even the entirety of the creature's blood at once can cure." Papa had lifted a finger, wagging it back and forth. "Caging an animal for such purposes, to drain its blood regularly, this I cannot condone."

He had argued against the use of such treatments, putting forth his own proposal: dragon stem cells. If a medication could be found—or synthesized—to suppress the innate immune system, there was a chance that permanent cures could be effected.

But his colleagues had brushed aside her father's hypothesis as nonsensical ramblings.

"They did," Luke said, snapping her back to the present. His knuckles were white as they gripped the mantle. "Once it was determined their medication had no effect on the virus, the scientists undertook a new approach, using rubber tubing to run blood straight from the creature's veins into my own."

"What!" Her jaw dropped in horror. "They ought to know better. Dragon's blood is far more acidic than ours. It must be neutralized—with the simple addition of sodium bicarbonate—before an infusion can be safely performed. Such a process could have killed you."

"They often came close." He pinched the bridge of his nose. "It was hellish. I swear I could feel the dragon's blood burn a path through my veins and arteries. My heart would race and I would struggle to breathe. All while a monstrous headache engulfed my skull with its vice-like grip. Sometimes seizures." He dragged in a deep breath. "That said, when the worst had passed, I felt better. Almost normal." He looked rueful.

"For how long?" His answer would be telling. The more ill a patient, the shorter the duration of relief.

"A week. Sometimes two."

Not long, then. But if he refused to stay, was it enough time to reach his brother? Regardless, a transfusion would temporarily stabilize his condition until the dragon eggs hatched. It would provide her with time to review Papa's notes, to consider if a cure was even possible. Her laboratory was equipped for chemical analysis, not cell biology.

He shook his head. "No. I see what you're thinking, Natalia. It's not right to ask that of Zia."

"One treatment." The possibility hung in the air between them. "With *neutralized* dragon's blood." She held up a hand when he began to object again. "You struggled to resist my sword attack on the flat ground of the castle courtyard. Yet you propose to climb into the highland mountains carrying a lit brazier and five dragon eggs? And when Rathail's hunter follows?" She shook her head. "I can't manage it alone. You need to be in fighting form. For Zia's sake—for the brood of dragonets on the way—let us help you."

~~~

His shoulders slumped under the weight of inescapable fact. Natalia was right. He wasn't physically fit enough to offer much help on their journey or even during a fight if they remained at Castle Kinlarig. Without time to rest and recover, he might drag them down. He only need undergo this treatment one more time. He was willing to endure the pain—for he doubted she could eliminate all the symptoms—if it meant seeing her, Zia and the dragon eggs safe.

And he'd be liar if he didn't admit that he was thinking of a night or two spent in her bed. At last. Their affair would—by necessity—be brief. He wouldn't saddle her with an ailing husband. But he wanted their time together to be memorable. And for the right reasons.

Except Natalia was an organic chemist, not a physician or even a biologist. He frowned, wondering if he was about to play pin cushion to her attempts. "You've done this before, transfused dragon's blood into a human?"

She darted a glance at her laboratory workbench. "It's more an infusion, the slow injection of a substance into a vein." Her voice was detached yet determined. He wasn't escaping this treatment.

"Not an answer, Natalia."

"No," she admitted on a sigh. "But I once helped my father do so by neutralizing dragon's blood. You're a cryptozoologist with anatomical knowledge. You've taken samples of her blood in the past, so if you direct the needle…"

He closed his eyes a brief moment, resigned. It *would* help. "Very well. Let's do it."

With a sharp nod, she spun on her heel.

While Natalia located a syringe, he lowered himself once more onto the rug beside Zia, a process that was more difficult than it ought to be. The dragon dropped her chin on his knee, staring up into his eyes with what he hoped was sympathy. "A brief prick of pain." He rubbed her head in apology. "I'll be as quick as I can."

As children, he and his brother had dreamed of working with large, dangerous animals, staging mock battles in which they saved all of Edinburgh from such terrors as giant spiders, vampire bats and feathered serpents. They'd upset their mother and disgruntled their father who wished them both to become staid, upstanding members of society. Bankers like him.

But John had become a gamekeeper for a wealthy gentleman, and Luke had taken a government position in hopes that the Crown held close secrets about far more exotic creatures than might be found on a wealthy gentleman's estate. He hadn't been disappointed.

With no living species existing on the British Isles, there was debate among the cryptozoology community as to the very existence of dragons. Nonetheless, news of sightings from far-flung corners of the globe generated much excitement and speculation as to their origins. Were they an emerging species—like the kraken—or merely rare, a breed hunted to the brink of extinction, surviving only by retreating into distant and harsh environments where humans rarely wandered? Regardless, most considered dragons mythological. He himself had firsthand knowledge of only one species, but if all were hunted with the tenacity of those in the Ural Mountains, they might well remain so. He couldn't protect them all, but he would do anything he could to ensure the continuation of this particular species.

"You've grown so beautiful in my absence, Zia." He skimmed a hand over her scarlet dorsal crest scales. Their sheen had intensified since he left. An indication of sexual maturity? He considered the eggs nestled in their heap of smooth river rocks and assorted treasures. Or perhaps motherhood? He'd missed the opportunity to observe the changes, though perhaps he was better off for not having witnessed Kinross's death. Luke suspected the enormous intake of protein and nutrients was responsible for triggering parthenogenesis. A curious thought to tuck away for future contemplation. "I'll do my best to make this quick and as painless as possible." He lifted her tail, tapping his fingers along its underside, accustoming her to his touch. Zia closed her eyes, enjoying the attention.

Natalia sat beside him and pressed a bottle of ethyl alcohol into his hand along with a ball of cotton. Her forehead wrinkled. "The tail?"

"The ventral coccygeal vein," he answered, swabbing scales with the disinfectant as his heart rate jumped. "Easiest place to draw blood. She didn't object the last time I drew blood to check her sulfur levels, but if you'll hold her snout—a precaution in the event she decides to snap at us for such an insult?"

"A tiny prick, *lapochka*," Natalia crooned to the dragon, carefully wrapping her hands around the dragon's snout. She met his eyes briefly, nodding her encouragement. "For Luke."

Zia jerked—but didn't fight—as he slid the sharp, steel needle between two scales. A second later, blood rushed into the syringe as he pulled back the plunger, collecting ten milliliters of red dragon's blood. More than enough. He pressed another ball of cotton to the injection site as Zia flicked her tongue, largely unperturbed. Handing the sample to Natalia, he reminded himself why this needed to happen. That vial alone would sell for thousands on the black market. The least of the cruelties that Zia would endure should Rathail manage to take possession of their dragon.

Spinning in a circle upon her carpet, Zia turned, dropping her head into his lap, demanding attention in reparation for injury. He obliged, happy to soothe his own regrets.

At her workbench, Natalia carefully measured a white powder out onto a creased square of paper, weighing it upon a microscale. Satisfied, she mixed the chemical with the dragon's blood in a crucible, then proceeded to remove tiny samples, using litmus paper to test the acidity of the solution. Twisting her lips, she repeated the procedure. When the color of the sample finally turned a deep green—rather than a yellow-green—she drew the neutralized blood into a new syringe.

She knelt beside him. "Ready?"

"Resigned is perhaps the better term." He rolled the cuff of his sleeve above his elbow and tied a tourniquet. A blue vein stood in relief against his skin.

Swallowing, she set her jaw and took aim with the needle. He loved that, her determined persistence, her refusal to ever surrender. But her hand shook ever so slightly and the angle of her approach ensured a miss. His heart swelled and the corner of his mouth hitched upward. Earlier she'd pointed the tip of a sword at him, now she struggled to jab him with a tiny needle. He wrapped his fingers about hers and adjusted her aim. "Have you ever done this before?"

"No." She swallowed.

"I'll guide the needle; you inject the blood." With his help, the sharp tip pierced the skin of his forearm and slid at an angle into his vein. "Good. Now press the plunger down."

She squeezed slowly, sending dragon's blood rushing into his blood vessels, then withdrew the needle. "Done." She exhaled, releasing the breath she was holding. "Do you feel anything?"

Not once in the Ural Zavód had a single scientist inquired about his comfort. If anything, Dimitri Kravchuk had taken a certain glee from Luke's pain as the foreign fluid coursed into his body, burning a path through his arteries to perfuse his tissues. Sadistic, when a few moments with a simple chemical could have alleviated all the pain.

Needing her close, he wrapped his hand about her neck, over the soft wool of her scarf, and drew her forehead against his, breathing in her sweet, spicy scent. Then, closing his eyes, he considered her question. No pain rushed through his blood vessels. His heart rate was stable, his respiration unaffected. "Nothing yet. Save the slight strengthening of a headache." An understatement. As they sat, an otherwise peaceful scene upon the hearth, his headache—one that never quite left him anymore—crept up the back of his head and sank its claws into his temples. "But I haven't slept much in the past few days." Another understatement. He'd been in a hurry to reach her side, sleeping only when exhaustion forced him to seek out a pile of hay in a nearby barn.

Setting aside the syringe, she stood and held out a hand. "Come. We'll discuss your plans for Zia and Sasha later, after you've rested."

"I'm fine here. On the hearthrug." The room he'd once occupied was at the other side of the castle over the kitchens. Too far.

"Nonsense. We'll begin as we mean to go on." A slight blush tinged her cheeks. "You'll take my bed. Alone this time."

He took her hand and rose, unable to remember the last time he'd slept upon a mattress that wasn't infested with one biting insect or another. "I'm filthy." The castle hadn't been modernized. In the past, he'd made use of the nearby river, but inside Castle Kinlarig, his only options were a wet cloth or a hip bath in cold water—water she would have to carry from the courtyard's well.

A half shrug. "There's an ewer and pitcher, but you might as well topple directly into bed. I've not yet sold all the extra sheets." Natalia pulled him toward the curving stairs that led to her bedchamber.

He followed, unwilling to resist, and when she yanked back the bedcovers and gave him a gentle shove, he fell onto her soft, feather-filled mattress with a weary sigh and closed his eyes. Much as he wished to tug her to his side, waves of exhaustion dragged him down. Later, after he'd rested.

She drew a blanket over him. "Luke?" Her words were a soft, warm whisper at his ear.

"Yes?" He struggled to crack an eyelid.

"I must ask." Her face was suffused with pain. "At the Ural Zavód, did you ever encounter one Dimitri Kravchuk?"

Luke cursed and his head pounded. So much for drifting into a peaceful slumber. "He's the bastard responsible for my suffering. He's dead now." Probably. He had planted a knife in the man's thigh and left him bleeding out on the floor. Far too quick and kind an end for such a monster. But even if Luke had been inclined to repay the man for all the pain he had inflicted, only a narrow window of time had been open to him. Luke had snatched the man's keys, unfettered his fellow prisoners and uncaged the dragon.

"Good."

Luke didn't care for the distant tone of her voice or the way she averted her eyes. "You knew him." A statement, not a question.

"Yes." Still as a statue, Natalia's face hardened. Her voice grew cold and ice crept into her eyes. "He was my father's protégé and would have been the logical choice to succeed him, to carry on my father's work."

"Your father's work," he repeated. Had Kravchuk turned unwanted attentions upon his mentor's daughter? "Did he hurt you? What aren't you telling me?"

"I've a lesson." She spun away, lifting a sword propped against the wall. "William. He acts as my eyes in the village and will have news of Rathail's man. Any sign of recovery, and he'll send warning. You can rest without worry." With a zing, she slid the sword into a scabbard, strapping both to the belt at her waist. She could defend herself should trouble return but, damn it, he wished himself fit to fight by her side.

"Kravchuk, who was he to you?" he asked, ignoring the vise that clamped about his skull. Though he was certain he wouldn't like the answer, he had to know.

Natalia slid a knife into her boot, then lifted fierce eyes to meet his. "A man I once thought to marry."

CHAPTER FIVE

Natalia rubbed her hand absently over the base of her neck beneath her scarf as she flipped through the pages of Papa's notebook, scanning his detailed records. Even now, three years later, evidence of her father's act of treason was still embedded in her very skin. Evidence of the unauthorized and reckless experiment that had restored her ability to walk, but sent her into permanent exile. His supervisors had been furious when he refused to explain what he had done with the dragon's eggshell after the hatchling crawled free.

Can I do this? No need to offer Luke false hope if she couldn't.

She was an organic chemist. Any and all biological knowledge she possessed had been absorbed at home, when Papa had rambled on about the propagation of "stem cells", a term first used by the German scientist Ernst Haeckel. Not her field, but a fascinating concept nonetheless.

Dragon's blood contained a scattering of rare hematopoietic cells. Those her father had been able to isolate only hinted at the potential of those stem cells he had cultivated from the extraembryonic tissues of Zia's newly-hatched egg. Cells he had used to cure his only child, Natalia.

True, the implantation of dragon stem cells came with unexpected—and not always welcome—side effects, but they also held out the possibility of curing the man she loved. *Loved.* Luke, the only man to ever capture her heart.

Out of tradition and convenience, she'd agreed to marry Dimitri Kravchuk, hoping they might one day grow to care for each other. Marrying the Laird of Kinlarig had been a desperate grab at a brighter future. Both had been a mistake. She'd not truly known either man, but Luke? Attraction had been instantaneous, but the friendship—and eventually love—had grown over the space of many months. For him, she would do her best to replicate Papa's work.

She possessed a fuge. The glassware, the pipettes and test tubes were ready and waiting. The reagents she could mix. She could even cobble together a makeshift incubator. But the growth media—a liquid that would approximate body fluids—was an impossibility. There was no choice but to skip the growth phase of Papa's instructions, using only the primary stem cells she could collect.

Movement caught her eye. William, out in the courtyard, had begun his warmup drills. Son of a local mill-worker, he'd stumbled upon one of her training sessions while delivering coal. The boy—young man, really—had begged for lessons. She'd agreed. With Luke gone, she'd needed a sparring partner, someone to keep her skills sharp in the event that her whereabouts would one day be discovered.

They had. But not until her own husband betrayed her. Her jaw tensed. It was proving impossible to set aside her anger at him, at Dimitri Kravchuk, as their sins continued to haunt her.

Natalia closed the notebook and tucked it back in a drawer. Once Luke was rested, they would need to discuss the possibilities and risks of such a treatment. Was she a fool to invite him to her bed—*push* him into it—when he'd yet to lay eyes on her concealed deformity? He loved Zia so very much, but perhaps he wouldn't want a woman who was part dragon—if only the tiniest fraction—in his arms. In his life. For that was what she wanted, wasn't it? To not just share a bed, but a life?

Regardless, she needed to show him, and soon. It would be irresponsible of her not to reveal the possible long-term and unpredictable side effects of dragon stem cell therapy. And if he turned away from her in disgust, well, that was his prerogative. His choice to reject the possibility of a complete recovery—at least physically—from his time in the Ural Zavód.

For now, she had a lesson to teach. She snatched up two swords, dull and blunted ones intended only for practice, then grabbed a third, sharpened rapier. William had earned it.

Striding through the great hall, her mind circled back to Dimitri Kravchuk. May his corpse rot in hell. To think she'd thought to marry him. When she'd fallen from the cliffs—moments after discovering the dragon's cave, a nest filled with eggs within—had he climbed down to her aid? No. Instead, he'd climbed up the last few feet to the cave and disappeared inside. While *others* attended to her on the ground, bracing her neck, carrying her home. Her fists tightened on the blades she held.

Not only had he not come to his mentor's defense when Papa broke protocol to save her—performing a procedure forever marking her as different—Dimitri Kravchuk had taken it as a personal affront that *anyone* dared touch any part of the dragon eggs which he himself had collected from the nest. He'd made her father's life a living hell.

Fearing they were to be sent to a *katorga* labor camp in Siberia for his actions, her father had bid her to pack. They were leaving, fleeing Russia, stealing away with Zia and Yuri—two tiny hatchlings—in hopes of establishing a breeding colony as well as his research on foreign soil. But Papa had never reached the train. Shot by their pursuers—guards who intended the same end for Natalia—he'd fallen, dead before his body hit the ground. Weeping, she had snatched up his notebook and run, leaping onto the already-moving train, determined to reach Scotland and carry out his wishes. But Yuri was sickly and—despite her every effort to keep the dragonets warm and properly fed—Zia alone survived the journey.

Without a male, there was no hope of a breeding colony. And so Natalia kept her secret—and Papa's notebook—carefully concealed. But now, with Dimitri Kravchuk the likely villain responsible for Luke's condition, it was time to dust off old, unhappy memories and turn them out into the light so that she could right the wrong done to him. To unwind her scarf and share with Luke the one story she'd never told.

Much had changed in the past few hours. She could at last see a path forward if only he would agree to her plans. Yet she needed to rein in her expectations. One step at a time, for there were numerous obstacles yet to hurdle.

"Lady Kinlarig?" Aileen's voice managed to be both subservient and disapproving at the same time. It wore on her nerves. "A moment of your time?"

Natalia stopped in the foyer. As it was connected to the kitchens, it was all but impossible to enter or exit the castle without Aileen taking note. "Yes, Aileen?" She pressed her lips together and braced herself.

With only four years between them, they ought to have been friends. As it was, they barely managed to occupy the same room. Resentment permeated their every interaction. Natalia—a foreigner of no consequence—had married the town's most eligible bachelor, simultaneously achieving the dream of every young woman in town and snatching away the very possibility that they might one day become the lady of the castle. No matter Kinross had been a miserable prize. Aileen disliked Zia even more, blaming the arrival of the dragon for ruining her life. The enforced secrecy of all activities within the castle made her existence a rather lonely one. Not once had Natalia seen her pet Zia, though of late the woman had made a few tentative overtures toward befriending the dragon. Perhaps out of fear of becoming her next victim?

"Shall I air out Mr. Dryden's former bedchamber?" Eyebrows raised, Aileen leaned to the side, looking behind Natalia as if expecting Luke to appear.

The rooms above the kitchen—the warmest in the castle—were currently occupied by McKay and his granddaughter. An unusual privilege, but given a mere three individuals lived within the castle walls and that her butler, McKay, was ancient and not in particularly good health, enforcing traditional servant quarters would be cruel. The bedchamber above theirs belonged to Luke. Or it had.

"Thank you, but that will be unnecessary." For years Natalia had confined her rebellions to wearing trousers and pressing ancient weapons back into service. If she wished to take a lover, why hide it? It wasn't as if Aileen took pains to hide her unchaperoned jaunts—not even from her grandfather—to the river's edge to meet her lover, now fiancé. "We do need to take more care with castle security. The gate was left unlocked allowing an intruder to reach the great hall. Given the recent attacks on the castle—"

"Attacks might be overstating it a bit, wouldn't you say?" Aileen interrupted on a sigh. "Was it really necessary to put an arrow through that man's shoulder? If you'd let Zia go, we could all move on to new lives." So much for Aileen warming to Zia's presence. "The Laird of Kinlarig sold the dragon. He was within his rights and given the creature ate him..."

A thought flashed to mind. How much had she shared with her lover? "You haven't told—"

"Michael?" Aileen crossed her arms. "Of course not. I swore to keep your not-so-mythical beast a secret, and I have. What he knows is that I've no interest in shouldering the role of old retainer tied to the estate by the tradition of generations. I'm to meet him soon, to discuss our wedding. You'll have to find someone else to manage the Edinburgh townhome. The financial situation here worsens by the day, and there's little hope of stretching supplies into the summer. I'm done."

"I'm sorry for that." Natalia felt an inexplicable upwelling of sympathy. The McKays had stood by her side through a rough winter without pay. "The bed hangings in Mr. Dryden's room are of exceptional quality, are they not?"

"They are."

"Take them." She waved her hand. "Take them all. The hangings, the sheets, the feather mattress and pillows."

Aileen's eyes grew wide. "Truly?"

There was no reason for them to be at odds, and Aileen *had* sacrificed much attending to both her grandfather and a strange, foreign woman with a dangerous creature in tow. She deserved a chance to build a life of her own, one not so solitary and lonely. "Consider them a wedding gift. I wish you all the best." Natalia didn't wait for a response. She had extended an olive branch. Aileen would either take advantage of the opportunity, or she would not. Her emotions were tattered and raw. Perhaps a bout with her student in the fresh air and sunlight would lift her spirits.

~~~

Consciousness swam to the surface, and Luke forced open his eyes. He pushed himself up onto his elbows before he could sink back into the warm, soft embrace of Natalia's mattress. He'd not slept so deeply in ages, nor felt so... normal. Despite that, the sun still hung high in the sky. He'd slept no more than a few hours. Amazing, the effects of a few milliliters of *neutralized* dragon's blood.

Telling that his Russian captor had deliberately chosen to torment Luke by skipping such a small—yet critical—step. He hadn't the slightest regret about killing Dimitri Kravchuk, not after all the tortures the man had inflicted upon him in the name of science.

Two years ago, deep lines of disapproval had carved themselves into the face of Luke's supervisor when he pointed out that British-Russian tensions were unlikely to resolve anytime soon and proposed to make the journey on his own, without any reliance upon or support from the department. Nonetheless, he'd been granted six months' leave, a small stack of untraceable bank notes, and a stern warning that the department would disavow any involvement.

Traveling up the Kama river to Perm, climbing into the Ural Mountains, Luke had entertained dreams of greatness. Of praise and accolades for his accomplishments in the field of cryptozoology by safeguarding the future of a rare species of Mountain Dragon. While he'd found numerous caves displaying evidence of prior habitation, locating an active lair had taken far, far longer than he'd hoped. And he hadn't been the only one looking.

All hope of a bright future had died the day the Russians captured him. Turned into a laboratory rat, the damage done to his liver by that vicious pathogen was irreparable. Whatever resurrection of good health this final treatment of dragon's blood had brought him, it wouldn't last. But he'd make the best of it while he could.

Both in and out of Natalia's bed. An opportunity for which he'd never dared hope.

Smiling, Luke threw back the covers and swung his stocking-clad feet over the edge of the bed. He pulled on his boots. A glance in a mirror revealed that the whites of his eyes were a most disturbing yellow. And he smelled. *That* he could fix. He rubbed a hand across the rough stubble of his beard. The judicious application of a razor wouldn't be amiss either.

Ignoring the ewer of water on a nearby table, he grabbed his rucksack, snagged a sword for himself and made his way to his old bedchamber above the kitchens. All was as he'd left it. He pulled a skeet pigeon from his trunk, dashed off a brief note explaining the situation and requesting immediate assistance from the department. After winding the mechanism, he tossed the mechanical bird from the window, praying it would reach Edinburgh and his supervisor without delay.

Luke grabbed clean clothes, a linen towel and located his razor. Passing through the kitchens, he snagged the extra key to the postern door and headed out. In the courtyard, Natalia trained a young man, making the adolescent work for every touch he won. He hesitated. Perhaps he shouldn't leave them here alone? No. He shook his head. There wasn't the slightest chance the hunter had recovered yet from his venom-laced claw wounds. He'd be lucky if those medieval arrows didn't cause sepsis. Regardless, Luke would wash quickly.

He slipped out the postern door, locking it behind him, and made his way down a path to the river's edge. Assuring himself there was no audience, he set down his rucksack and stripped bare. He tossed his clothes across the hull of an overturned boat that sat on the riverbank, half-consumed by weeds, then waded in, quickly applying soap and razor before making his way onto the shore to dress.

As Luke climbed back toward the castle rubbing the towel over his hair, the unmistakable sound of lovemaking met his ears. He must have veered down a different fork of the path.

There was a gasp of horror, and he yanked away the cloth, turning, attempting to cast his gaze down— anywhere but at the two lovers. Alas, he failed.

Aileen half-sat upon a moss-covered wall of a rubble-strewn ruin with her skirts hiked up about her waist. A man, his arms wrapped about her, his trousers undone and shoved low about his hips, lifted his mouth from her neck. Both faces flushed with interrupted lust and embarrassment.

"Sorry. So, so sorry." And he was, very much so. Not once had he ever wished to gaze upon Aileen's bare bosom. Jaw slack, he began to turn away—except the man's face was familiar.

A scene flashed to mind. Luke upon his knees while guards surrounded him, each pointing a loaded musket at his chest. Their captain striding over the cave's rocky ledge, barking questions in Russian that he hadn't understood. A strike to the side of his head that had split his lip and dropped him to the ground. Rough manacles biting into his wrists as he was dragged away. A key turning in a lock, imprisoning him in the Ural Zavód. *This* was the man who had stolen his freedom.

"You!" Luke tossed aside his rucksack and drew the sword slung upon his hip, retreating as fast as the uneven and root-tangled ground allowed. But a single infusion of dragon's blood could not undo all the damage of those endless months locked inside the Ural Zavód. He was at a decided disadvantage.

Misha Ivanov—Aileen's lover—also drew a blade. A shorter, curved knife. He lashed out. Only the man's need to pull up his trousers kept his knife from slicing through Luke's throat.

"Michael!" Aileen called, yanking her bodice back into place and flapping at her rucked skirts. "Stop! He's... a friend."

Ivanov ignored her, crouching low as he circled around Luke, looking for an opportunity to strike. And found it. He lunged, slashing his blade at Luke's stomach.

Luke deflected the attack with his sword. *Clang.* Reverberations jolted up his arm, jarring his shoulder and nearly making him lose his grip. This would end badly. Ivanov's skills might not be on par with Natalia's, but this former soldier was also stronger, murderous, and completely devoid of empathy.

Again, Ivanov rushed toward him. This time, luck wasn't on Luke's side. He blocked the worst of the strike, but the tip of the curved blade sliced through his shirt, through the skin of his left bicep. A sharp tear of pain. Blood, warm and sticky, soaked his sleeve.

He stumbled. The next slash came hard upon the last. There was no chance he could win this fight. No chance he'd survive to warn Natalia that Rathail's hunter wasn't the only threat. The Russians had ferreted out their location.

His face an emotionless mask, Ivanov swung his blade down toward Luke's shoulder. A teeth-rattling screech rent the air as their blades slid past each other and caught at the hilts. Arm shaking, Luke struggled to hold off the Russian. With every last ounce of his strength, he shoved the man backward.

A fleeting victory. Ivanov's lip curled, and he lunged forward. Luke leapt backward, but his foot caught upon a tree root and he fell. Exposed.

"Michael!" Aileen ran forward, stumbling to a halt before her lover, her arms spread wide. "Please. Luke won't," she blushed a furious crimson, "say anything about... about what we were doing. Not to my grandfather or anyone else." She glanced over her shoulder. "Will you?"

Sad, that he'd been reduced to hiding behind a woman's skirts, grateful for her defense. He and Ivanov had crossed blades but three times and his chest heaved with the effort. Had he refused the dragon's blood, he'd already be a corpse upon the path. He clapped a palm over the gash in his arm. The cut was deep enough to require stitches.

"Of course not." Luke himself would do his best to wipe the vision of the Russian mixing work with pleasure from his memory. His concerns lay elsewhere. If Ivanov had been in the village long enough to seduce Aileen, then he wanted more from Natalia than her dragon.

Shit.

Ivanov lowered his arm. "You are certain?" *Almost a convincing Scottish accent.* A man who could blend into his environment so well was more than a mere guard.

"Go," Aileen said. She stepped closer and kissed her beau on the cheek.

His free hand fell upon her hip, and he pulled her close, whispering into her ear, all while keeping a close eye on Luke. Her face paled, but she nodded. Ivanov slid something from his pocket and pressed it into her hand. She swallowed, then tucked the item into a small pouch tied at her waist.

Releasing her, Ivanov slid his knife back into its sheath and stalked over to Luke's rucksack. He opened it and proceeded to examine each item within as if it might be a direct threat to his lady love. But there was only one item inside that held any value to Luke. And, damn him, Ivanov found it. With a nasty grin stretching across his face, the Russian pulled out the paper packet of milk thistle seed, flicked open its paper flap, and dumped the contents onto the ground.

Luke cursed, but dared not raise further objection.

"Nothing." Dropping the rucksack to the ground, Ivanov looked to Aileen—his inside woman—and nodded. "You will let me know if he causes you any trouble?"

"Immediately."

With a brief kiss to her lips, the Russian took his leave, disappearing around the bend. He stalked off into the forest, headed who knew where. Worry twisted Luke's stomach. Two men in this corner of Scotland with an interest in dragons was two men too many. Without assistance, escaping the castle unnoticed would be difficult if not impossible.

Aileen stooped to stuff Luke's possessions back into his bag. "I'm sorry. My fiancé is fiercely protective. You rather took us by surprise." Her face was bright red, and she didn't meet his eyes.

He stood, slowly and painfully sheathing his sword. Imagining Ivanov as protective of anyone but himself made him shake his head. "Fiancé?" he repeated. He tore a strip of cloth from the hem of his shirt, cringing as he bound the bleeding gash. A makeshift bandage until he could locate a needle and thread.

"Grandfather will warm to him," she said, catching Luke by his elbow and leading him along the path. "Soon, when Michael concludes his negotiations to invest in the textile mill upriver, we will marry."

Luke glanced at Aileen. Her chin was lifted and her shoulders pulled back. Proud and working hard to convince herself such an event would come to pass. Determined enough that she'd let Ivanov—*er*—lift her skirts in the woods, an unwise risk. He should warn her—would warn her—*after* he'd spoken with Natalia. For now, he would watch his words around the young woman.

~~~

"Hold it higher," Natalia instructed William, expecting she might regret teaching him this maneuver. Though she'd given their practice session her all, he'd bested her twice today already. Not only had he grown three inches this past winter, his body had begun to take on the hard, angular planes of manhood. "Turn your wrist a touch to the right. Yes, like that. Now thrust the blade toward your enemy's bowels."

"Like this?" William lunged at the straw figure set up inside the courtyard.

"Exactly like that." There wasn't much more she could teach him. Regret tinged her smile. She was proud of her student but needed to terminate their lessons. Not only did Luke's arrival mean she needed to plan for their departure, it had drastically altered her plans for today's laboratory work.

Her last set of experiments had indicated that she was close to synthesizing a modified version of dragon's venom, but something about the structure was wrong, possibly the isomerism. But she'd come closer to unlocking its exact composition than she'd ever managed in Russia when her supervisors had rolled their eyes at her efforts—heart disease, why work to treat the useless elderly?—but tolerated her because of her father, whose brilliance was much prized.

Luke's health came first, and he had no need of a drug to lower his blood pressure. So instead of refining dragon's venom—a purification process useful both for her research and for coating the tips of arrows— she needed to assess, then rearrange and adapt her equipment to suit a cell biology project.

"That's enough for today," she said.

Would her father be proud of her, or horrified that she'd held back his breakthrough from the scientific world? She tugged at her scarf, wishing she could unwind it and toss it away. Too long she'd been hiding, protecting secrets inside thick stone walls. Her life in Castle Kinlarig was a lonely one. Luke's renewed presence had served to underscore that fact. And though she did not wish to return to Russia, she missed interacting with like-minded scientists. Here—in a quiet corner of Scotland—she was cut off from all news of innovations in her field, from all academic conversations that might inform her own work.

Not that she wished to abandon Zia, but with assistance, with someone else to oversee the dragon, she would be free to travel to Edinburgh, to rejoin the research world and learn what advancements had been made while she was hidden away. She longed to take on another project—one not tied to dragons—so she might discuss her work and publish her findings.

Shoulders slumping, William held the rapier out—hilt first—to her.

Reflexively, Natalia reached for it. Then stopped. "Keep it."

"Truly?"

"Truly." With a nod, she continued. "You're ready. That fencing studio you wish to open in Edinburgh? If your uncle was serious about allowing you to work for him, to set up a studio in the back of his warehouse, it's time. You've my permission to take a selection of weapons and armor from the great hall."

William's grin nearly split his face in two, but his excitement was quickly followed by suspicion. "Why?" His eyes narrowed. "Are you leaving? Did something happen to your dragon?"

A few villagers had guessed the truth. Mostly children as they were the ones able to set aside disbelief. She'd caught a few prowling the castle grounds, hoping for a glimpse, but William had taken it one step further. He'd pestered McKay—a great uncle of sorts—to allow him to work within the castle walls from time to time, assisting with all the odd jobs that required more strength than the butler had left to him.

Natalia wagged a finger back and forth. "You know nothing about such a creature. Hush." Only a promise of lessons in swordsmanship had convinced William to stop pestering her with questions about dragons... and to discourage other young visitors. "There's a man in the village who wishes to capture her. I cannot let that happen, and so I must leave to take her elsewhere."

"But you promised I could meet her someday." His voice held a hint of a boyish whine. "And if you're leaving..."

So she had. "Let me see what I can arrange."

As per her agreement with the Department of Cryptozoology, she kept Zia carefully hidden away in the laboratory whenever William—a non-resident—was inside the castle's walls. But they'd terminated her funding, so perhaps such strict secrecy was no longer binding. After all, William had made himself as essential as McKay and Aileen.

"About that man," William began, his voice eager. "The one you shot an arrow through, he might have an assistant now. There's a new hunter in town. I can follow him to the pub tonight, find out why he's here."

An assistant? The tiny hairs on the back of her neck rose. "No. Stay away. Far away."

"I'll only listen..."

"I'd rather you not become tangled in whatever—" The postern door opened and Luke and Aileen entered. She'd seen them both leave, but individually. Her eyebrows drew together. Both looked rumpled and— Luke was bleeding. Her heart leapt into her throat, and she had to choke back a cry of distress as she rushed in their direction. William followed behind her. "What happened?"

Luke glanced at the young man and frowned. "A small disagreement with Aileen's fiancé." He pressed his lips together and gave a small shake of his head.

Aileen's mouth flattened. "He was defending my honor."

"William," Natalia said. "Time to go. Be certain McKay locks the castle gate behind you."

"Aww," William objected, but he turned and did as his fencing master bid him, proudly carrying away his weapon.

Wrinkling her nose against the noxious odor of the thin, watery soup—cabbage with parsnips this time— simmering upon the surface of the stove, Natalia set a tea kettle to boil. "Have we any whisky?"

"Some." Aileen placed a sewing kit upon the table, dropped a rag beside it, then—twisting her lips in disapproval—fetched the bottle. "But from the look of his eyes, Mr. Dryden's liver is pickled enough." She crossed her arms and frowned. "What is it with all the swords? Have none of you ever fired a pistol?"

"The antique weapons in Castle Kinlarig were collected for display," Natalia answered. "No one thought to stock gunpowder or the appropriate bullets. Items hard to justify on a restricted budget. Not to mention the alarming possibility of a misfire. Such old weapons are unreliable."

"Swords still function when they're wet, and one needn't stop to reload," Luke added, grimacing as he rolled his sleeve above his wound. "And mine was taken from me..." He lifted his gaze to Natalia's.

In the Ural Mountains. She didn't need him to say it aloud.

Pouring the last of the whisky into a glass, she dropped the needle and thread into the alcohol before blotting Luke's arm. The wound wasn't too deep and, despite the mud on his trousers, he smelled clean and fresh, like clear river water. A vast improvement. She slid her gaze sideways. Aileen, other the other hand... "Care to explain what happened?"

Aileen's bodice gaped and strands of hair floated loose from her coiffure. Color rose high upon her cheeks. "Michael was taken by surprise and overreacted. Nothing to fret about. Mr. Dryden will be fine."

A gross understatement, given he required stitches. Luke's immune system was already compromised. An infected wound was the last thing he needed. But she bit back the comment. "Did Michael at least agree to call the banns?"

Shifting on her feet, Aileen looked away. "We were about to discuss that when—" She shoved a handful of cloth strips into Natalia's palm. "You have this under control. I need to..." Hand flapping, she fled the kitchens. Natalia laughed. "Did you catch them—"

"I did." Luke pulled a face. "Horrifying enough, but we have another problem." He craned his neck to be certain Aileen was out of earshot. "Her fiancé's name isn't Michael, it's Misha. Misha Ivanov."

CHAPTER SIX

She glanced up sharply. "Misha Ivanov. A Russian."
Her heart began to pound. *They'd found her.*

Two years ago she would have questioned the presence
of any man who wandered so freely about the edges of her
property. But when Aileen mentioned he was in the wool
industry and negotiating to purchase cloth produced at
the mill upstream, Natalia had dismissed him without
another thought. Stupid of her.

"You're being watched," Luke said. "Closely. Do you
know him?"

Natalia shook her head. "No. We've not met. Nor is the
name familiar." Though her insides had turned to jelly,
the cut in his arm required her immediate attention. She
took a deep breath and pinched the two halves together.
"How—exactly—do *you* know him?" She braced herself
for the answer.

"He was the man who caught me, a guard from the Ural Zavód." Luke hissed as the sharp steel bit through his skin, but he didn't move. "No, more than a guard, though I'm not certain what to call him. Agent? Spy?"

"No mention of me or Zia?" She slid the needle through his skin. A second stitch. It steadied her nerves to count them.

"None." His teeth gritted against the pain, and he fell silent.

Luke had taken pains to cover his tracks and would worry he'd led the man to her gate. On that count she could reassure him. "Michael—Misha Ivanov—arrived in town a few months ago, perhaps a week or two before Lord Kinross's death. He can't have learned about my presence from you."

"Thank aether."

Three. Four. It was done. She tied a knot. Blotted the wound once more, then wrapped a strip of cloth about his bare arm. Only then did she allow her mind to churn. Rathail's hunter and now a Russian spy. First one, then the other. She voiced her suspicion aloud. "If Rathail made it known that he would soon come into possession of a Russian Mountain Dragon..."

"Word might have reached Russian ears." Luke swore. She agreed with every profane word that fell from his lips. "Easy enough to send an agent to investigate," he continued, "to dally with the castle's pretty, young housekeeper."

With the recent financial difficulties and Lord Kinross's death, Natalia could well understand Aileen's hopes for marriage. Who wouldn't want to flee? "She was an easy target."

"Ivanov's Scottish brogue is very convincing," Luke agreed.

She frowned. In two months' time, Ivanov had made no move against Zia. Or her. Or even Rathail's man. Had Luke not stumbled across him in the woods, his presence would have remained undiscovered. What could he possibly—

"Come." She turned on her heel and strode though the great hall to her laboratory. Zia's head lifted, her golden eyes tracking her movement as Natalia rushed across the room to yank open a drawer. Safe. Papa's notes were safe. Only then did she realize she was shaking. She'd not bothered to secure them. No one here knew about the experiment, and they were written in Cyrillic. But a Russian now lurked outside her castle, quietly insinuating himself into Aileen's life. A dragon and a person might not be easily transported, but a handful of research notes? Easily pilfered by a lovestruck housekeeper.

That explained Aileen's tremulous overtures. She was terrified of Zia, especially after Lord Kinross's grisly death, and for the past six weeks, the dragon had rarely left the laboratory. Ivanov had convinced Aileen—against every instinct—to befriend the dragon that guarded the secrets he wished to steal. Or perhaps just to copy. Why go through the effort of dragging home two fugitives if the science was unsound? She wasn't safe, not even inside her own home, not when Aileen could be so easily seduced.

"Natalia?" Luke's voice was soft, concerned. "Is something wrong?"

"No, but I—" She turned, about to share her revelation, but lost her voice. Luke had closed the door to the laboratory and unbuttoned the collar of his shirt. She stared at the hollow of his bare throat. How much time did they have left to them? Alone? With a bedchamber only a flight of stairs away? "It's nothing."

It wasn't. But it could wait a little bit longer. A few inches deeper, and his wound would have been far, far more serious. She watched, her mouth dry, as the two halves of his shirt fell apart, while he peeled the ruined garment from his torso and tossed it upon the flames of the fire burning steadily in the grate.

Kinross, for all his superior breeding, hadn't been a gentleman at all. While not cruel, he'd cared not a whit for her pleasure, only his, and what it bought him. Her first time with a man had been a disappointment.

It had, however, been enlightening. Luke—she was absolutely certain—wouldn't leave her bed before she was well and truly satisfied.

"Natalia?" Heat crept into his voice.

"Mmm." She licked her lips, unable to tear her gaze away from his bare chest where, despite his illness, muscles still rippled as he prowled across the room to stand before her. His trousers hung low upon his hips, a sheathed sword still strapped to his belt.

"You're staring as if you've never seen a man's chest before." A corner of his mouth twitched upward, and his dark eyes flashed.

She hadn't. Not really. Removal of clothing wasn't necessary to consummate a marriage. But this was about pleasure, about their mutual desire, and she wanted to *see* him.

"An entire year, fencing a hot, sweaty man, and not once did he ever remove his shirt." She ran an experimental fingertip over the curve of his clavicle, and he stepped closer.

"You were married." He brushed his lips across hers.

A shiver of longing ran across her skin, humming as it dove deeper and sparked every nerve ending to life. Her breath came quicker. "No longer an obstacle. But your wounded arm might be."

"It's fine." Another kiss, this time to the corner of her mouth, then to the edge of her jaw. Soft and teasing. "Besides, I've waited years to touch you." Broad hands landed upon her hips, pulling her snug against his obvious desire. "There's no reason we need wait for darkness to fall, not when I want to explore every inch of your skin. Slowly."

Every inch. She swallowed and pushed at his chest. Something fluttered low in her stomach. It was time, time to uncover her secret. "Wait."

He tensed. But he stepped back, his eyes questioning. "I thought—"

"Correctly." Rising onto her toes, she pressed a kiss to his lips. "But there's something you need to see first. Come." She lifted her father's notebook from the drawer then, without meeting his gaze, climbed the stairs to her bedchamber and dropped the yellowed pages upon the table. She closed her eyes for a brief moment and took a deep breath, praying he wouldn't recoil in horror.

She turned about to find Luke waiting patiently, despite his frown and the questions written across his face. He lifted an eyebrow as she untied the knot of her scarf.

"I don't wear it to honor tradition." Taking a deep breath, she pulled it from her neck and turned away, exposing her nape, allowing him to gaze upon the strange scales that grew from her skin. Shaking, she awaited judgment. This was a moment of truth. Would he be repulsed?

"Aether," he breathed. "How? Why?"

She glanced over her shoulder but saw nothing except curiosity and awe. "The real reason I had to flee Russia." How to sum up such a defining moment in a few succinct words? "I fell from the cliffs—dragon egg hunting—and broke my neck."

"Broke?"

"I never would have walked again, save my father refused to let me die. When one of the eggs hatched, he broke every rule and took an enormous risk, collecting and transplanting cells he isolated from the extraembryonic membranes that remained behind inside the dragon's eggshell. Stem cells, he called them, undifferentiated cells capable of becoming, repairing... anything."

"And it worked." Luke let out a low whistle as he moved closer. "Impressive. May I touch?"

She nodded, relieved he didn't consider them an aberration of nature.

The rough pad of his finger skimmed across a scale, sending a shiver down her spine. "You can feel that?"

"Yes. They're a part of my skin, a part of me." She held her breath, waiting. "Most of them are clustered about the lower cervical vertebrae—where the grafting took place—but dragon stem cells possess a migratory inclination..."

"There are more?" His warm lips pressed against the scattering of scales at her nape, sending a rush of heat through her entire body. "Might I resume explorations?"

Still worried, she half-turned in his arms, studying his face. "If you're certain you wish to continue."

A low laugh escaped him, his breath hot on her neck. "Never doubt it, Natalia." His fingers released one of the clasps that held her corset closed. "I'll have questions later." Another fell open. And another. "Many." The leather parted, hanging from its narrow straps at her shoulders. "But for now, my only goal is to make you pant my name while you—"

"Luke," she whispered as he flicked open the button of her waistband and tugged her chemise free. His palm skimmed upward over the soft curve of her stomach, her ribs, until he cupped the weight of her breast.

"It's a start," he murmured against her neck, then nipped at her skin. "But I'm aiming for a much louder cry." He raised both arms at once, pulling off her chemise and corset vest in one smooth motion. His fingers trailed down her vertebrae, one by one, following the path of the dragon scales. "So beautiful, my dragon lady."

Beautiful?

With a soft laugh, she turned to face him and began to toy with the buttons that held the fall of his trousers closed. "You find them... attractive?"

"Incredibly." His voice was low and rough. "They're a part of you."

She loved him so much, had missed him so much. "When you didn't return—"

"You were in my thoughts every single day." He caught her lips for a long, slow kiss. "Never daring to hope you would ever be free." His fingers stabbed into her hair, into the braided twist wrapped about her crown. "That you could ever be mine."

"Not free, perhaps," she whispered. "But yours ever since you first lifted a blade against me."

With a low rumble of a laugh, he brought his mouth down. Their next kiss was hard, possessive, a tangle of tongues as they claimed each other.

Slowly, step by step, he walked backward. Until he bumped into the base of her bed. Large, soft and canopied. But there would be no drawing the curtains closed.

He moved away, pulling off boots, stockings, trousers while she did the same. She stared, taking in the magnificent length of his member as it sprang free, dark curls at its root. Reaching, she cupped the sac that hung beneath. With a low growl, his arms were around her, tumbling her onto the mattress, naked, as they gave themselves over to hunger and need. The peaked tips of her breasts brushed the crisp hairs of his chest as she shoved her fingers into this thick hair and kissed him with all the passion she'd locked away for over three years. The press of his hard length against her soft thigh left her breathless and wanting oh so much more.

She slid her hands down his back, admiring the tight muscles that flexed beneath his firm skin—until she grasped his buttocks. Spreading her legs, she dug her nails into their flesh and yanked him closer.

The low groan from the back of his throat let her know he approved of her touch. And yet he pulled away, trailing kisses down her body, his lips sucking at the tips of her breasts, teeth nipping at their tips before nibbling lower, ever closer to that pulsing, aching center between her thighs. He spread her legs wider.

"Luke!" she cried, when he parted her folds, taking her in his mouth, his tongue stroking her small sensitive nub as his hands slid up and down her thighs.

So close. So close, and yet she wanted—needed—more. She pushed at his shoulders, tugging at his hair until he lifted his face, his eyes glassy. "Luke, please. I want you in me. Now."

He crawled up her body, his eyes hungry, and braced his heavy weight on his elbows. She wound her arms around him and pulled him to her, closing her eyes to commit the feel of his body to memory. He notched his cock against her wet opening and she slid her legs upward about him, wrapping them about his hips. A hot, thick pressure pushed into her. Slowly, easing into her channel, deeper and deeper still. Stretching her.

She looked up into his eyes and saw tightly wound control, self-restraint balanced on a knife's edge. He was giving her body time to adjust, treating her as if she were fragile. But it only made the need build, made her want more. She flexed her hips, and he moved deeper inside of her. Such exquisite fullness.

Then he cupped her face, took her lips with his and began to move inside her. Gently at first, then thrusting harder, faster. Spirals of pleasure circled around and through her body, their coils tightening. Gasping, she tore her mouth away to focus on the need gathering where they joined, where friction built to glorious heights as he drove into her again and again.

With a sudden flash, fire ignited, racing across her skin, sending her entire body into an exquisite convulsion. "Luke!" Spasms tore through her as she ground her core against him, dragging forth every last ounce of pleasure of her climax.

Poised above her, the muscles of Luke's neck and arms strained as he drove into her chasing his own release. Beautiful and all hers. With a roar, he thrust deeply, once, twice, then pulled free, spending himself—hot and wet—upon her belly.

~~~

Sated, relaxed and happy, Luke lay beside her, relieved he'd had the presence of mind to withdraw. Taking her to bed had been everything he'd ever dared hope for. But still he wanted more, wanted her for himself, this amazing woman. He never wanted to let her go. But his would be a short forever. She deserved a chance to change her mind, to leave—unencumbered—should his condition become too much to bear. Already, the cut to his arm ached more than it ought, a reminder that this lifespan would be short.

He'd followed Natalia up the curving stairs, distracted by the alluring sway of her hips, without the vaguest notion of what she was about to reveal. Dragon scales. A side effect of a miraculous treatment. She'd broken her neck, but lived, even walked again, her health completely restored. Already he'd been breathless with anticipation, but to find she hid yet more wonders had stolen away his last breath.

"Twenty-one months and twenty-three days," Natalia whispered.

No accusation surfaced in her voice, rather a wistfulness, reminding them of all the time they'd lost. He pulled her against his side and pressed a kiss to her hair. "I should have told you, even though you would have threatened to run me through." He'd been so naïve, so confident as he left on his quest. "I wanted to take advantage of the summer months. To fetch a dragon, then return with my prize for the lady of the castle." For the woman he loved but could never have, not completely.

"But the Department of Cryptozoology turned you down." Natalia frowned. "As they should have."

"They did." He cringed at the memory. "Repeatedly. But I kept pleading the case for establishing a dragon sanctuary on British soil and, eventually, my supervisor agreed to let me go. An unofficial and deniable one-man expedition into Russia." He'd left immediately. A boat to St. Petersburg. A train—via Moscow—to Perm. From there hiking into the mountains.

His mind drifted back to the raw beauty of the pine-covered mountains, to the quaint villages tucked in their valleys. Carrying his gear upon his back, he'd slept in the wilderness, enjoying the solitude, the freedom, traveling by foot into the peaks of the Urals.

"I found a cave. A mother with two dragonets scampering about her feet. Young, but too old to easily transport to Scotland." Quietly, carefully, he'd backed away from the cave. "Armed men swooped in. Too many to fight." He closed his eyes. "They killed the mother, penned the dragonets. Perhaps I should be grateful I was not killed as well."

He opened his eyes to find her above him, her blue eyes bright with passion. "I, for one, am grateful that you were not."

During his captivity, he'd often lost hope and simply wished for it all to end. "But for thoughts of you, I might have given up. I was no better than a laboratory rat." He brushed a hand over the surface of her braid. She claimed it kept her hair up and out of the way, but Luke thought of it as her golden, shimmering crown.

He'd not yet had the pleasure of uncoiling, unbraiding its twists. Imagining the glory of such hair spread across her shoulders as she rode atop him made his groin stir with approval.

"Go on." Captivated by his story, she searched his eyes for more.

Doing his best to ignore the soft press of her bare breasts against his chest, he continued. "After they decided I knew nothing of interest, I was injected with an unknown pathogen, thrown in solitary confinement, and left to endure the fevers that followed. From time to time, they would drag me into the infirmary and I would catch glimpses of the two dragonets in cages, miserable and defeated, their blood used for a scattering of 'treatments' that did little to improve my condition. I lost track of time."

A tear ran down her cheek. "Finish," she whispered.

"There's not much more to tell." He offered her a faint smile. Delirious with fevers half the time, much of the time had been a painful blur. "My Russian improved. A little. Enough to understand that this past winter a spy was captured in Germany. Secrets had been spilled, and an entire research facility north of Moscow had to be shut down. As a precaution, all biotechnological research was being relocated." Her eyes widened for she had worked within the extensive network of corridors and rooms that comprised the Ural Zavód. "In the chaos an opportunity presented itself. I left a man for dead. And escaped with a dragon."

"Dimitri Kravchuk," she said, her voice flat. "Good."

"You were to marry him." Luke seethed at the thought. What had the man done?

"I was young and foolish." Her face contorted as she rolled away to sit upon the edge of the mattress. "Not once did he visit me after the... accident. Not so much as to hold my hand while the village doctor informed my father there was nothing to do but measure his daughter for a coffin."

Letting out a low hiss from between his teeth, Luke pushed himself upright and wrapped his arms about her, glad he'd ended the man's life.

She turned her teary-eyed face toward him. "Any love he professed was a lie. Or secondary to his desire for advancement. My father broke the rules to save me, and Dimitri reported him. The treatment had worked, and we had to flee. Lest he end in prison, and me under a microscope."

Much as Luke had. "Dimitri, did you love him?"

"No." She shook her head. "My father wished for me to marry his protégé. There was no one who had captured my heart, so I agreed." A tear slid down her cheek. "But for his actions, my father would still be alive."

They sat—silent—for a long moment, taking comfort in each other's arms. Luke silently vowed that neither of them would ever fall into Russian hands. Not them, not Zia or her eggs, and certainly not her father's notations.

"Notations," he said aloud, his gaze lifting to the table across the room. "The laboratory notebook."

She swallowed and nodded. "And dragon eggs about to hatch. If I follow his protocol, collect the stem cells from the membranes inside their shells, there's a chance I can cure you. Permanently. There are certain risks, but..." Her eyes pled with him to let her try.

"A cure?" He all but forgot to breathe. He'd accept almost any risk for a permanent cure.

"It means we can't leave the castle, can't head for the Trossachs." She pressed a hand to his chest. "Not yet. Everything I need is here."

She slid from the bed and pulled her chemise over her head to guard against the cold of the bedchamber where no fire burned. But its neckline gaped, revealing the sexy scattering of scales at her nape, and its hem skimmed the back of her thighs, below the curve of her arse. One glimpse of her backside, and the wanting—the need—began again.

Already half-hard, he climbed from the bed and dragged on his trousers before crossing the room to peer over her shoulder at the old notebook—thin for such an important treatise—filled with brittle, yellowed pages and words inked in Cyrillic. Luke knew only a smattering of Russian, picked up by listening to what little conversation filtered down the hallway. He couldn't read a single word.

"All of Papa's work, everything he accomplished in that one-week time span beginning the night Zia emerged from her egg, is here." She tapped on the notebook. "I've kept Papa's secret—my secret—because I cannot be certain it will not end up in the wrong hands."

"And cause an extinction by sending an army of unscrupulous men into the Ural Mountains hunting for dragon eggs." And it would, if this miracle she promised was truly possible. "A week." He shoved his fingers into his wild hair. "Maybe two. That's a lot of time to wait." He'd hoped to leave Castle Kinlarig much, much sooner. "Waiting, with Ivanov and Rathail's hunter circling, seems unwise."

"But we should stay." She dropped the notebook and began to pace, her face flushed with excitement. "With you restored to health, we can travel at will. An opportunity like this might never happen again. When Zia's eggs hatch, I will have an abundance of material. But I can only collect the stem cells, I can't culture them. I've not the proper equipment—an incubator—or growth media to allow them time to replicate. I'll collect those I can. Inject them all."

"Into my liver." He lifted his eyebrows, curious. "To divide and grow inside me?" He'd endured worse. If this was the path to a cure, he'd follow it.

"It's the only way." She ran her fingers over the back of her neck, tracing a fingertip over the edge of a scale. "There will be side effects as they engraft." She looked at him. "Unpredictable side effects. And you'll need to take a few doses of a horrid drug to prevent zenograft rejection. But dragon cells divide quickly and integrate thoroughly. They'll replace damaged tissue, restore connective tissue, and commingle with existing cells. You will be healed."

"Healed." Was it possible? He hardly dared hope.

"Dragon stem cells defy explanation. Did you notice how quickly Zia recovered from the Voltaic prod burn?"

True. As they'd passed the dragon while she guarded her clutch, there'd been no sign of the charred scales. Instead, the spot bore new scales, ones that were a slightly lighter shade than those that surrounded them. He whistled. "A matter of hours." His skin tingled. Would he grow his own scales? He rather hoped he would.

"It's why I've not handed over Papa's notes to the Department of Cryptozoology. He knew the British would be unable to turn him away, not with such knowledge— and two dragons—in his possession. But..." Her voice trailed off as a distant look passed across her face.

"He was killed..."

A quick nod. "I decided to withhold such knowledge until I'd thoroughly evaluated my new employer. When they handed me a useless husband, paltry funds, and a cold, damp castle, I decided I did not wish to place the power of dragon stem cells in the hands of a government, any government." She shrugged. "Besides, without a male, without dragon eggs, the entire project was an impossibility."

"And now?"

"I find myself breaking my own rules to save a man." She pressed a soft kiss to his lips. "This will, of course, go to your head."

It rather did.

He wanted this. He did. So badly it hurt. "Safer to

leave," he said, meeting her gaze. For her, he was willing to delay—even forgo—the treatment. "For you, Zia and her brood. If we can reach the Trossachs, there will be future opportunities." *If.* He wasn't at all certain he was capable of helping her fend off an attack, especially on the move.

"Healed!" Natalia poked a finger into his chest to emphasize her point. "Permanently. No more need of milk thistle tea or dragon's blood. *That* is worth the risk. It's worth every risk." She wrapped her arms about his waist and tipped her face upward. "If not for yourself, consider my own selfish wishes to keep you with me, in my life and in my bed, for years to come."

Warmth spread over his heart. "If that is what you want."

"It is."

A low, soft hiss slithered up the stairways. A yelp and a thud. Then a sharp cry.

Natalia snatched up her sword and took off down the curving, stone stairs.

"Wait!" Luke called, following. Too late. He caught a glimpse of her white cotton chemise as she leapt into her laboratory, sword at the ready.

CHAPTER SEVEN

"Lady Kinlarig," Aileen cried, terrified. "Call her off."

Luke rounded the last of the stairs to find the dragon hissing, her teeth bared and her tongue flicking as she took slow steps toward the woman. Her leathery wings extended, readying for an attack.

"Zia, no," Natalia ordered, her voice firm, but she still gripped her weapon. "Come."

With great reluctance, the dragon stilled, then folded her wings and turned away, stalking back to stand beside the fireplace, her body tense and on alert. Defending her brood.

He prayed Aileen knew nothing about the dragon eggs. Luke moved to stand beside Natalia. Silent, but holding his own blade.

"What brings you to my laboratory, Aileen?" Suspicion threaded its way through Natalia's voice, and with good reason. It was a well-known fact that Aileen disliked Zia and avoided her at all costs. Except, now there was the question of her Russian lover.

"Might it have anything to do with this?" Luke bent, scooping a yellow lump from the floor and holding it aloft. "Sulfur. A bribe for the dragon. Is this what your fiancé handed you when he whispered in your ear? What, exactly, does he want you to locate?"

Aileen lifted her chin. "I've no idea where that came from." She flapped her hand at a tray upon the laboratory workbench, shifting toward the door. "You left the tea kettle boiling, so I..." Her gaze flicked between Natalia and Luke, only just realizing how very little they wore. A furious red blush stained her cheeks. And then her gaze fell upon Natalia's bare neck.

Natalia slapped her palm over the few scales that crept from the edge of her neck onto her shoulder.

"I'll go now." Aileen bolted from the room.

Luke stalked behind Aileen, shoving the heavy wooden door closed. Turning, he leaned against it. The throbbing in his arm wasn't lessening. "That rather confirms it. Ivanov is after your father's notes."

"And finally convinced her to ferret them out. I'll keep them close from now on." Natalia pushed shut a drawer that was cracked open, then turned her attention to the tea set that rested upon her workbench. "Not once has Aileen ever brought me tea. How could she possibly think we wouldn't find her behavior suspicious? Yet we've barely eaten today." She poured a cup of tea, sniffed it, then took a sip. "It's fine. No point in poisoning us before she's found what she's after."

He closed the distance between them, taking a warm potato scone folded in a napkin from her hands, his mind on anything but food. The cotton of her chemise hung loosely over the peaked tips of her breasts, a seductive reminder of recent activities. He shifted, half-aroused, tempted to ignore their situation a few more hours, to lead her back to bed, to bury himself deep inside her once more.

With a smile that invited him to do exactly that, she rose up onto her toes and pressed a soft kiss to his lips, leaving him breathless with desire.

Thunk.

The sound came from the direction of the fireplace. Both of them turned to stare at Zia, who had plucked an egg from her nest and dropped it upon the floor. The dragon lifted her head, blinked her golden eyes once, then turned her attention back to her brood, nudging aside rocks and other treasure pieces, gently taking each egg in her mouth before rotating it into a new position. Satisfied, she lowered herself onto her belly beside them, then cocked her head slightly as if daring them to comment on her actions.

Dammit. So much for sex.

Frowning, Natalia set aside her tea cup to lift the solitary, gold-streaked egg from the cold, flagstone floor.

"It's still warm. And the shell is intact." She crouched beside Zia, then pushed aside stones and treasures to tuck the rejected egg deep into the dragon's hoard beside the others. "Why would she do that?"

A frisson of worry skittered down his spine. "It's thought dragons will push non-viable eggs from their nests."

Natalia added more coal to the fire burning in the grate, as if more heat might convince Zia to keep all her eggs. "You think something is wrong with that particular egg?" She stroked Zia's head. Instead of relaxing into the attention, the dragon remained alert.

"Possibly. Time will tell." He could hear the strain in his voice. Too quickly he'd latched on to the hope of a cure that dragon stem cells might offer. If something was wrong with the eggs, that hope could be snatched away in the blink of an eye. He forced himself to explain. "Parthenogenesis is not a common way for a vertebrate species to reproduce. All five eggs might well be non-viable."

And he did wish to live, to fight off the disease that now all but defined his life. His cirrhotic liver, yellow-orange and riddled with disease plagued him daily. He snorted. An unappealing organ, that one gave no thought until it ceased to function properly. Only then could one arrive at a true appreciation for its many duties.

Remaining at Castle Kinlarig was a risk, but his tangle with Misha had underscored the sad fact that not even dragon's blood had restored his strength enough to successfully help Natalia defend against an attack while transporting Zia and her eggs.

Still, logic argued that Natalia's treatment and recovery might have been a fluke, a one-time miracle enacted by a renowned, experienced cell biologist, a remedy they were incapable of reproducing with limited resources and experience. Especially if the eggs were non-viable. Had Zia—much like chickens without a rooster—laid a clutch of unfertilized eggs? Was it nothing but instinct for her to stand guard? So little was known about the reproductive habits of the rare Russian Mountain Dragon species.

"Is there no way to know?" Natalia's eyebrows drew together. "If none of the eggs will ever hatch..."

Then hope for a cure must be abandoned and alternate plans made. "We could try candling."

"Candling?"

"A way to look inside developing eggs. Hold the egg against a bright and concentrated source of light—not necessarily a candle—and it's possible to see blood vessels and a shadow of the embryo within."

"So an unfertilized or infertile egg—" She crossed her arms which pulled her chemise tight across her glorious breasts. Aether, he wanted nothing more than to take her back to bed and finish exploring every last inch of her skin. She caught the direction of his gaze and plumped her breasts up further, throwing him a sultry look.

His lips started to twitch. But he needed to focus on science, not sex.

He coughed, cleared his throat, then choked out a response. "Will appear mostly clear, perhaps with some spots beneath the shell. But first," he pushed a firm note into his voice, "we need to dress. Not only is it impossible to concentrate with such beauty before me, it's cold, and I'm beginning to worry yet more visitors might arrive."

She sighed. "A regrettable possibility."

A few minutes later, wrapped once again in cotton, wool and leather, they stepped back into the laboratory. While Natalia hunted for a working decilamp, Luke crouched beside the fireplace, crooning sweet nothings to the dragon as he held out the lump of sulfur, hoping to coax Zia away from her nest. Unsettling to think how well Ivanov knew his way about dragons.

Zia pushed onto her feet. She took a hesitant step toward him, then paused, turning back toward her treasure hoard. *Shit.* Again the dragon began to shift the stones. Tongue flicking, she touched—tasted—each egg. Then with the tip of her snout, she rolled an egg back onto the stone floor. Then another.

His heart sank.

"Still in working order," Natalia called, giving the small device in her hand a final forceful shake to fully excite the bioluminescent bacteria within. "Faint, but it brightened after I injected a little substrate into the gel chamber." Her gaze followed his to the floor and her face fell. "Not promising."

Not at all, but hope twisted in his chest, begging for a chance. "Let's have a look before we make a pronouncement?"

While Zia watched, he lifted the first rejected egg, its gold streaks glimmering in the lamplight. Natalia brought the light to the tip of the dragon egg, and the interior illuminated. One end glowed a deep red, the other a golden yellow. A network of blood vessels threaded beneath the surface.

Luke exhaled, letting out a breath he'd not known he was holding. "Blood vessels indicate it is—or was— viable." He pointed at the dark red end. "The embryo is here. The light space at the other end is the air sac."

"So it's viable?" Hope flared in her bright eyes.

He was about to say "fertilized" but stopped himself. Parthenogenesis. "It might be, but it's awfully small for a six-week-old egg. Unless the dragonet within moves as we watch, we can't be certain." But they couldn't return the egg to Zia's nest. "We'll keep this egg separate but warm, then watch to see if it continues to develop."

For now, he placed the rejected egg on the hearth on the far side of the coal fire—close enough to keep it warm, but far from Zia's nest—and stacked a number of warm river rocks about it.

The movement sent a shooting pain through his arm, one that radiated out from the cut Ivanov had dealt him. Infected? Already? They'd taken care to sterilize the needle and thread. And less than two hours had passed since he'd returned from the river. Far too soon for an infection to flare. Something wasn't right.

When he straightened, Natalia already held the decilamp against the shell of the second rejected egg.

"Mostly clear and golden, but there's a small, darker section." She looked up with sad eyes. "The embryo died?"

Drawn in, he nodded. "This," he pointed at a circlet of red beneath the shell, "is called a blood ring. It forms when the embryo dies and the blood vessels detach from the interior of the shell. From the small size of the fetus, I'd say this one died some time ago."

Zia pawed at his leg, dragging claws down the leg of his trousers. Her tongue flicked in and out and her tail thrashed.

"I think she wants it back," Natalia said. "But whatever for?"

He shrugged and set the second, non-viable egg down before her. The dragon lifted the egg in her mouth, flutter-hopped a few feet away, then dropped it to the floor. She lifted her forefoot and brought it down swiftly and decisively upon the egg. *Splat!* The contents oozed from beneath her feet. Soundly rejected.

"Zia!" Natalia scolded.

"No." He snatched up a rag and bent to mop up the mess, cringing at the pain in his shoulder the movement caused. "It's good instinct. A rotten egg—one incubating harmful bacteria—can destroy the whole brood." Luke wondered if she would seek out the second egg, but the dragon returned to her nest, settling down once again into sentry position.

"What of the remaining three?" She lowered herself onto the rug beside Zia, absently stroking her head.

• *106* •

"Should we candle them as well? I never considered parthenogenic eggs a possibility. After Kinross's death, I thought her refusal to leave her treasure hoard, her constant pestering for me to light a fire, was shock. I should have investigated further. Had I known, I would have kept the fire burning, helped keep a closer watch over her eggs."

Likely the large *meal* Zia had made of the laird—with unusually high concentrations of nutrients and calories—was the environmental trigger that stimulated the atypical reproductive strategy. No need to enlighten Natalia with that grim thought. He sat upon the floor beside her and took her free hand in his. Though small and elegant, it was also skillful and strong. And demanding. Whether it gripped a test tube, a sword or—his heart gave a great thud—him, she was a rare find of a woman. Decisive, leaving no one in doubt of her intentions. And yet so fragile underneath.

An accident had broken her spine, and the treatment forced her to flee Russia, bringing about her father's death. And now his own country had failed her, relying too heavily upon a so-called gentleman who thought only of himself and refused to answer her repeated requests for help. Yet still she blamed herself for the outcome of a rare reproductive event that might have been compromised by improper incubation?

He frowned, unwilling to let guilt define her memory of this moment. "How could you possibly have known? Zia hid her eggs well. Besides, who in their right mind would dig into a dragon's treasure pile without good reason or permission? You're not responsible for this situation."

Her laugh was bitter. "Am I not? But for me, my father might be alive, we might be in Russia, and you would not be ill."

"Stop." He squeezed her hand. "I count it a rare privilege to have met you, to have worked with a dragon I consider a friend." All he wanted was to see her, Zia and her brood safe.

Lie.

With one foot in the grave, he'd somehow managed to convince himself that would be enough. But the moment she'd dangled the possibility of a cure before him, everything had shifted. He wanted to be with her. As her lover, as her husband, as the father of her children. But though he might feel relatively well at the moment, his health would eventually begin to fail. He would become a burden. Unless...

He stared at the eggs nestled inside the dragon hoard. If they weren't viable, he and Natalia ought to make plans to leave immediately. But if they were—he glanced at the sad-eyed beauty beside him—then he was willing to wait, to serve as laboratory rat one last time.

~~~

It ought to be cozy, sitting before a fire with Luke, holding his hand while, outside, day faded into night.

But instead of dreaming of a future together, she was brooding over the past, over things that could not be altered. Too long she'd existed in such a state, tied to a dissolute, opportunist of a husband who had done nothing save foist the care and keeping of his family estate upon her while pilfering from governmental funds earmarked for *her* research.

Free at last, it was time to take decisive action to secure a better future for herself. Luke in her bed was only a beginning. She wanted more. So, so much more. But if there was no cure for his illness, her dreams of spending a lifetime—hers—with him would crumble, slowly but surely. Every hope she had for their future hinged upon a viable egg.

"I can't wait," she said. "The uncertainty will kill me." She reached out to touch the tip of a half-buried egg, then addressed Zia. "May I?"

Zia nudged her hand toward her brood, as if proud to have her offspring admired.

She pushed aside a brass doorknob and a few stones before placing her fingertips upon an egg. She looked to Zia. No objection. Gently, she lifted an egg free, careful to keep it near the flames. Luke handed her the decilamp, and she touched the light to the shell of the egg, illuminating its golden-red interior.

Within a large mass of dark red shifted.

"It's alive!" she gasped.

"And nearly ready to hatch." His voice held a note of excitement, but it was tempered with relief. Or was that apprehension?

One by one, they examined all three eggs. All contained viable embryos. Three dragonets due to hatch in less than two-weeks' time. She looked to Luke with a grin, but her smile fell away as she studied his face. "What's wrong?"

He gave a quick shake of his head. "Nothing."

She frowned. "You doubt my laboratory skills, my ability to culture stem cells? It's true, I have no formal training, and I didn't help Papa with the original experiment." She'd been flat on her back in a bed, wondering when she would die. "It is a risk. My plan might well fail."

Luke shifted, touching his fingers lightly to his injured arm, then dropping them away, clearly uncomfortable. He drew a deep breath. "It bothers me that Ivanov is out there, scheming..." He shook his head. "I want the cure. But I also want you safe. And I'm certain Ivanov—now that his true identity has been discovered—won't wait two weeks before pressing his agenda."

Nor was she. But to step beyond the castle walls was to expose themselves to capture. By Ivanov or Rathail's hunter. Even if they altered their plans, fled for the city and somehow managed to reach Edinburgh, once they arrived, what then? Bone-deep, she knew men in formal attire would swoop in—citing various rules and regulations—snatching away Zia and her clutch. Without a newly-hatched dragon egg or access to a laboratory, all hope of curing Luke would be lost.

And *that* was unacceptable.

"We need to stay." She closed her eyes and forced the truth from deep in her heart. "Three years ago I fell in love with a man I couldn't have. My feelings haven't changed, but my plans have. I want more than a few years. I want a lifetime. I'll do everything—anything—to cure you." Snapping open her eyes, she pinned him with her gaze. "Give me that chance?"

"Natalia, I—" Luke swayed, nearly toppling to the floor.

She caught him about the shoulders and pressed a palm to his brow. Only minutes before he'd seemed fine, but now he was hot. Feverish.

"My arm." He unbuttoned his shirt and shrugged it from his shoulder. "It feels infected."

Already? Her mind raced. How was it possible? They'd been so careful. And the dragon's blood should have helped quell any complications. Eyebrows furrowed, she unwound the bandage and gasped. Red, inflamed streaks radiated from the wound, and pus oozed from beneath the threads that pierced his skin. "Aether, how?" This was no simple infection. Something more was going on.

He cursed. "I might not make it two days, forget about two weeks. It was that damn sword of Misha's. A polluted sword."

"Polluted?"

He grimaced. "Some guards in the Ural Zavód carried them, blades dipped in a brew of noxious bacteria and allowed to dry. A single nick can be deadly."

No. Absolutely not. Her heart flipped over and began to beat irregularly. She would not lose Luke to a bacterial infection. She jumped to her feet and ran to her workbench, snatching up a bottle of ethyl alcohol, a scalpel and a clean cloth. Kneeling at his side a moment later, she said, "Brace yourself. This *will* hurt."

Luke dragged in a deep breath and held it. He gave a short nod.

As the stitches fell away, a thin, yellow-green liquid trickled down his arm. A lump formed in her throat as she pressed at the inflamed tissue, draining it, trying to maintain a calm demeanor when she wanted to cry out in alarm. She needed to clean it, kill as many bacteria as possible so that his immune system had a chance to fight the infection. She poured a measure of ethyl alcohol directly into the open wound, and Luke hissed and spat a long string of colorful curses, some in Russian. Concerned, Zia nudged his thigh.

"A most interesting prison vocabulary." Her voice shook. A feeble attempt to inject a certain lightness into her voice, despite the growing panic that tightened like an iron band about her chest. The wound was angry and septic, a ticking bomb. She set the bottle aside—an easy arm's length away—before loosely wrapping a clean cloth about his upper arm. "We'll try that again in an hour's time."

Luke slumped, pale. "We need a new plan." He looked at her with tired eyes. The hollows beneath his cheekbones seemed more pronounced. "I sent a skeet pigeon to Edinburgh, to the Department of Cryptozoology. There's a faint possibility they might send help."

He was making plans for her, plans that wouldn't include him. She opened her mouth to object. Closed it. If this infection proceeded apace, he would be unfit for travel in a matter of hours. Her heart jumped. With fear for him, with fear for herself. She'd not traveled anywhere, not since fleeing Russia three years past.

"It's possible," he began. "If you exit through the postern door and—"

"Lady Kinlarig!" Aileen pushed the thick wood of the door open, stumbling into the room. "Two pteryformes!" She pointed at the window set into the stone wall and flapped her hand. "With men upon their backs!"

Natalia ran to the window, and her jaw fell open. Silhouetted by the setting sun, two human forms— mounted upon the creatures' backs and holding reins— swooped low above the castle.

One such beast had been circling the town for some time now, but that was not uncommon in this part of Scotland. Zia would often peer out the window at it, hissing, perhaps envious of another reptile whose wings were strong enough, wide enough to lift their entire body into the sky. But they were *wild* beasts. Natalia had never seen one with a rider. Until now. *Aether!* Had Misha Ivanov *flown* into Scotland? And who rode by his side? She'd thought herself safe behind stone walls and bolted iron gates, but if a man could saddle and ride such a creature such barriers wouldn't stop him. She tried to swallow her mounting panic.

"It can't be!" Aileen grabbed her arm. "*Michael?*" Shock and denial were at war in her voice.

"Misha," Luke corrected as he made his way across the room, slowly, and with great effort.

"Your sword-wielding, *Russian* fiancé, Misha Ivanov." Ice dripped from Natalia's voice.

Stupid of her not to insist upon meeting the man, but Aileen hadn't offered. Of late, Natalia had put special effort into avoiding her more than usual. The humming and the slight skip in her step as the housekeeper worked had been irritating, exacerbated by the smug and pitying smiles Aileen had bestowed upon her—the poor Lady of Kinlarig, young widow.

"He's only following orders!" Aileen backed away, and though she defended her intended, a certain stricken look stole across her face. Did she just now realize a man such as Misha might not return her loyalty? "*You* stole the dragon. The papers..."

The pteryform riders circled back, lower this time. Clawed feet extended, they landed with grace *inside* the castle courtyard. Dismounting, their two riders shoved flight goggles upward upon foreheads and waited.

Ice crystalized in Natalia's veins as she recognized one of the riders. Mouth open, she gaped at Luke. *How was it possible?*

Luke cursed. Not just because their unwelcome visitors arrived fully armed and garbed in leather, but because Ivanov was accompanied by one Dimitri Kravchuk. "How is he not dead?"

Natalia grabbed a sword. She added another blade to the belt at her waist and slid one into her boot, one that she could throw.

Tiresome, this constant state of alert. The lairds of yore had armies. All she had was an ill—if determined—man and a dragon. Not only did Zia not breathe fire, her scales weren't impenetrable, and she couldn't fly, not really. Though her poison glands, sharp teeth and claws were quite effective at close range.

"You can't mean to confront them," Luke objected. He stabbed his fingers into his hair, fisting them as he shook his head in disbelief.

"What else am I to do?" She met his gaze with her eyebrows raised. "If they knock from *inside* the castle walls, McKay will open the door to them. Do you think the haughty disdain of a seventy-year-old butler will deter them from their plans?" She snatched up her scarf and wound it around her neck, concealing the dragon scales. Her mistake to have thought the cloth no longer necessary. "Perhaps I can buy us time." She pinned Aileen with a look. "Stay with Mr. Dryden. Be quiet. Do *not* alarm Zia." Stiffening her spine, she marched off to battle.

CHAPTER EIGHT

Outside twilight had fallen and the moon rose over the hills. In the distance, a bell rang. A gentle breeze brought in the crisp, cool air of the nearby river and ruffled a carpet of snowdrops. A peaceful night.

Elsewhere.

The main keep of Castle Kinlarig rose six stories, its curtain wall forty feet. It boasted walls that were six feet thick and a surround of defensive earthworks. But when the enemy could fly above it all to land within the courtyard, withstanding a siege became an impossibility. What point in hiding? Better to fully understand the situation she faced. Natalia pushed open the door and descended the stairs to stand before her enemies.

The air vibrated with tense hostility.

She detested both men. With his sword, Misha Ivanov had wounded Luke, perhaps fatally. But Dimitri

Kravchuk? His presence made her blood boil. To turn on his mentor, to not lift a finger when armed guards hunted her and her father with loaded weapons. To stoop so low as to forcibly inject an unknown virus into a healthy man so that he might *endeavor* to cure him with untreated dragon's blood. To think she'd once thought to marry the blackguard.

Ivanov—well-muscled and gripping a curved sword—stood a step behind Kravchuk, his face carefully blank as he awaited command. Not a man she could imagine bending on one knee to propose to a love-struck Scottish lass.

Dimitri, dressed in a leather flight jacket and trousers with a sword strapped to his side, looked no less lethal. His handsome face was familiar, but his eyes were cool and appraising. Her last glimpse of him had been from a distance, as she lay immobile upon a makeshift litter while men carried her away from the rocky base of the dragon cliffs. Did he now marvel at her ability to stand, to walk, to lift a sword?

Behind him, the two enormous beasts dug claws into the gravel and stretched out their long necks, huffing clouds of sulfurous breath into the wind as they spread their leathery wings wide. The keratinous skin covering their chests was thick, dark and... burnt? The rumors had been true, then, that her Russian colleagues in Kadskoye had succeeded in bioengineering a military-grade beast. A worrisome development.

"Control your beasts," Natalia demanded, refusing to cower before them, no matter a simple command could end her with one snap of their sharp beaks.

With a quick motion of his hands, Dimitri signaled to the two creatures behind him. With a final flap, they folded their wings against their sides and settled onto the ground, reluctantly obedient.

"What do you want?" Natalia planted fists on hips. Aggressive posturing that was completely unenforceable. Should they choose to force the situation, to attack, she would not emerge the victor. But, *by blade's edge*, she would make them regret the effort.

At Natalia's brave—and perhaps foolish—challenge, Dimitri smiled. "You need to ask?" It was a grin that had once charmed her and convinced her father to serve as his mentor. Until he'd abandoned her broken body, then betrayed the man who wished only to cure his daughter. "My betrothed, there was no need for you to run." His accent a reminder of her homeland, yet so very unwelcome falling from his lips. "Your father alone broke the rules. We've searched for years, but the British government hid you well. Until Rathail made it known that his catalogue of goods would soon include a certain rare species of dragon."

Silently, she cursed her husband's name.

Dimitri took a step forward, and she lifted her sword. "I am not your betrothed, you cold-hearted, opportunistic bastard. Not so much as a word of sympathy reached my ears as I lay dying." She spit on the ground. "No, you were too busy exploiting the opportunity, crowing over *our* find, over the dragon eggs we located *together*. Carrying them back to the Ural Zavód, watching over them, celebrating the hatchlings. What did my father do, save to use the scraps you tossed away to attempt a cure?"

"One that worked." He took another step forward, one with a slight hitch. Light spilling from the castle's interior glinted off ice chips deeply embedded in his frozen eyes as he assessed her form. "One that ought to be shared."

Her fingers twitched with a need to claw the arrogant expression from his face. "With you? A man who betrayed the woman he professed to love, all so that he might crown himself director of dragon research?" Natalia shook her head. Her heart had been right to save itself for Luke, the polar opposite of the man who stood before her. "Go. When you ordered my father killed, you destroyed the only man who could give you the knowledge you pursue. Go. Leave me in peace. There's nothing here for you."

"There's a dragon." Dimitri's eyes narrowed. "A Russian dragon. One that a man named Rathail seeks to sell, piece by piece upon the black market, an unacceptable end."

Agreed. Though she refused to voice the shared sentiment.

Dimitri flicked a hand, and Ivanov strode to his pteryform's side to unknot a rope fastened about the neck of a large, canvas sack. The body of Rathail's hunter slid free and slumped onto the ground with a soft *thud.* A dark, clotted gash gaped at this throat.

Ice shot through her body and, for a moment, she forgot to breathe.

"It proved impossible to convince him my claim to the dragon was stronger." Dimitri's eyes warned her she faced a similar end if she refused to cooperate. "Agree to hand over your father's notations and assist the dragon into its cage," he waved a hand toward the corner of the courtyard where Kinross had met his untimely end attempting to force a hungry dragon behind bars, "and I will leave you—and your lover—to enjoy the damp and cold of this indefensible pile of rocks. The walking dead are of no concern to me."

A cold sweat broke out over her skin. He knew of Luke's wound and approved. Another inconvenient man who thought to block him from acquiring something he desired, easily swatted away. How many bodies littered his path? "I have no notes, no record of my father's work." But she couldn't deny Zia's presence. Her hand tightened on the hilt of her sword. There was little hope of a peaceful resolution.

"Please." Dimitri cocked his head, ignoring her implied threat. "You don't truly expect me to believe that, do you? Ivanov attempted to extract them from you peacefully, to cultivate a friendship with Rathail's hunter. Alas," his grin grew sharp, "my intended had developed a certain amount of bite. He was right to send me word, if only that I might look upon you and fully recognize your father's brilliance."

"Michael!" Aileen ran down the stairs and into the castle courtyard, heedless of the tension, sparing not the slightest glance for Natalia, Dimitri, the pteryformes or the dead body that lay at their feet.

As she rushed past, the sleeve of her dress caught at the scarf loosely wrapped about Natalia's neck. As it fell open, Natalia clutched at it with white knuckles. Too late. She held her breath, suppressing a scream. Luke was right; meeting with them face to face had been a mistake.

Dimitri's visage brightened. "No record of your father's work?" He leaned forward, eyebrows raised. "Not written, perhaps, upon paper, but upon your skin. I must amend my original offer. Both you and the dragon will be returning to Russia."

"I married the Laird of Kinlarig. I'm Scottish now." She'd be damned if she would be dragged back to the Ural Zavód where scientists would tie her to a gurney and biopsy her spine, uncaring of her pain and agony as they sought to unravel the process by which Papa had restored his daughter's ability to walk.

"What is this about you working for the Russians?" Aileen cried, falling against her lover's chest, clutching at the cloth of his shirt and searching his face.

Dimitri rolled his eyes skyward. Amusement and disdain twisted together as he addressed Ivanov in Russian. "Swept up in a bit of local skirt?"

"You know as well as I the value of pillow talk," he answered, still in Russian, ignoring the woman who clung to him.

Aileen's mouth fell open, gaping at the foreign words that dropped from his lips. "It's true, you're Russian?"

"Any long-term interest?" Dimitri asked Ivanov.

He shook his head, his next words the only hint that a cold lump of clay hadn't replaced his heart. "She's harmless. Grant her and her grandfather safe passage."

"Done."

"Speak to *me*." Aileen pressed her hands to either side of Ivanov's face, forcing his gaze to her. "Don't do this. We have plans. I'm carrying your child! We *must* marry."

"He *has* a wife," Dimitri stated bluntly, switching back to English and addressing Aileen directly. "You see the impossibility."

"A wife?" Aileen dropped her arms, backing away and pressing a hand to her chest as if the truth sliced through her heart with a rusty, burred edge.

"It's true." Jaw set, Ivanov unhooked a pouch from his belt and held it out. "For the baby."

"No." Aileen sobbed as tears ran down her cheeks. "No, we have *plans*. Don't do this to me."

Much as she disliked the woman, Natalia's heart wept. She snatched the purse—heavy with coins—from Ivanov, then gently took Aileen's elbow, drawing her away. "I'm so sorry. Come back inside. We'll figure out what to do."

"All this emotion is exhausting and pointless." Contempt tugged at Dimitri's features. "Do we have an understanding, Natalia? Will you agree not to resist repatriation for the chance to save your lover?"

Luke's life for hers? The choice was easy. But for her, Luke wouldn't be ill, wouldn't be dying. If she cooperated, dosed him with enough dragon's blood, he

ANNE RENWICK

could smuggle the dragon eggs to Edinburgh. Someone there must speak—*read*—Russian. With Papa's notebook in hand, a scientist might be able to undo the damage done to Luke's liver. Cured, he could later take the young dragonets to his brother, to the refuge in the highlands.

But only if she sacrificed herself. And Zia.

Luke would never agree to such a plan.

Nor would she. Not until all other options were exhausted. She pushed Aileen toward the castle, then lied through her teeth. "We do."

"Wise decision." Dimitri snapped his fingers at the pteryformes, and they rose, stretching their wings and tossing their heads. "Enjoy your final night together, but pack your bags. It's time to return home."

~~~

Luke uttered a soft curse as the pteryformes and their riders disappeared into dark clouds that blotted out the moonlight. They'd be back, but for now, a brief reprieve had been granted. He'd half expected Ivanov and Kravchuk to force their way past Natalia and storm the castle, swords drawn. Especially once Aileen rushed out into the courtyard, exposing Natalia's secret. Kravchuk had been far too interested in her neckline. A bad omen.

His mistake for stabbing Dimitri in the leg. He should have driven that knife into the man's heart and given it a violent twist.

"Aether!" exclaimed William. Natalia's young student had *not* gone home. He'd snuck back into the castle and now stood beside Luke, gaping, his hand wrapped about the hilt of a sword. Of late, a rather standard pose here, even within the castle. "That dead man is the one Lady Kinlarig shot full of arrows this morning! Who, exactly, are the men *riding* pteryformes?"

Luke wasn't certain if the young man was shocked or impressed.

Rathail's hunter had fallen from a canvas bag and lay motionless upon the ground, a bloody gash at his neck. He was still there, a dark lump in the middle of the courtyard. Natalia had been right to drag Aileen away.

"No one you wish to meet," Luke said, sagging against the wall. In the short time Natalia had been gone, not only had his body temperature soared, but William had entered the laboratory claiming McKay had ordered him to deliver coal, a task that would take him conveniently close to the fireplace and a certain not-so-mythological dragon.

But Luke was too feverish, too worried to protest. He hadn't even been able to stop Aileen from rushing from the room, intent upon confronting her lover. Every last ounce of his attention had since been fixed upon events unfolding in the courtyard. Now, with the danger aloft and out of sight, William was full of questions.

"It *is* real," the young man whispered, halting a respectable distance away from Zia, awestruck. "From what I heard in the pub, I thought it would be bigger."

Question after question poured from the boy's mouth. The dragon, it seemed, was not at all a well-kept secret. Not after Rathail's hunter had arrived and begun asking questions. "And its wings are puny. Not a chance it can fly. Can it at least breathe fire?" He stepped closer, peering at the fireplace. "Are those eggs buried in a treasure hoard?"

No point in denying what William could see with his own eyes. Besides, he wielded a sword with skill, and his loyalty to Natalia might yet be useful. If Luke could no longer assist her, perhaps William could. Though the thought of setting such a young man against the likes of Ivanov and Kravchuk troubled him. "It's female," Luke answered, blinking. "She can't fly, not really. Only males—which are twice the size—spit fire. They've a kind of thermite in their crop." He pressed a hand to his forehead. His arm throbbed, and he was burning up. "Eggs, yes."

William glanced about. "Where's the other dragon then?"

"There isn't one. Not here."

He tugged an ear. "But she laid eggs."

"It's complicated."

The door cracked and William—clutching a sword— dropped into the *en garde* position. With a glance toward Luke, he lifted his blade. "Who goes there?"

"William?" Natalia stepped into the laboratory, frowning. "I thought I told you to go home. It's not safe here."

"I came back to help you save the dragon." William lowered the sword. "To warn you that the man you shot an arrow into had gone missing." He glanced at the window. "He's dead now, but he spent most of the day in the pub convincing the villagers that you don't deserve to be Lady Kinlarig, that they ought to help him chase you and the beast from the castle."

Wonderful. First Rathail's hunter. A pair of Russians. And next a mob of villagers carrying torches and pitchforks? The room tipped, and Luke eased himself down onto a bench, focusing his gaze on the floor in the event it decided to rush up at him.

Natalia crossed the room and knelt beside him to press a palm to his forehead. The level of worry in her eyes rose to a new level. "They want me to surrender Zia and my father's notes." She swallowed. "And myself."

"Not happening." Luke caught her wrist and pinned her with his gaze. "Don't even think to try it."

"Er." William shifted from foot to foot. "Can I... pet the dragon?"

"Yes. Carefully." Luke dug the lump of sulfur from his pocket. "Approach her slowly, let her taste your hand, then offer her this treat. If she hisses, back away quickly. If she spits venom, it will hurt. Badly."

"Venom? Fearsome!" William took the sulfur, then set about winning the friendship of the dragon. A few minutes later, they were fast friends. He knelt upon the carpet, stroking Zia's head while the dragon basked in his worship, eyes closed, a low, rumbly sound vibrating deep in her throat. The dragon shifted forward, resting her chin on his knees. William flashed them a grin.

"I gather there won't be a wedding for Aileen and Ivanov?"

Natalia followed his gaze to the pouch of coins tied to her belt. "A poor substitute for promises. Aileen's intended has left her in," she cleared her throat, "a difficult situation."

"A bairn on the way?" William asked bluntly, all ears.

Natalia winced, but nodded. "She's a bit distraught at the moment. When her senses return, I'll give the money to her." She glanced at Luke. "These developments complicate our situation."

Understatement of the year. "We need to send her and McKay away. Far away. In a manner that will not link them to our... quest."

"I could take them with me to Edinburgh, drop them off at your townhouse," William offered.

"With you?" Luke asked.

"Fencing and ancient swordplay techniques are all the rage." William puffed his chest. "Lady Kinlarig is allowing me to take a collection of weapons to the city. I've plans to open a fencing studio."

"Perfect." Luke straightened on his bench, trying to ignore the dull, vague pain that was settling in beneath the right side of his ribs. The infection must be triggering a relapse. He dragged in a steadying breath. "Pack a crate full of weapons, load it into the steam wagon. As pteryformes are nocturnal, you'll leave at dawn. When they catch up to you—and they will—you answer any questions they ask. Cooperate without a fight. Do I make myself clear?"

Though he nodded, William asked the obvious question. "But what of *you*? You can't stay here, alone to fight those men and their beasts. You're ill. Lady Kinlarig wields a sword, and the dragon is amazing, but she's not... well, she's too small to put up much of a fight. I mean, if you were caught off guard, like the laird, but..." The young man trailed off, realizing that he'd said too much.

"We have plans," Natalia said. Pain rippled across her face, and she glanced at the dragon eggs. An egg cracked open would provide the membranes she sought, but likely at the expense of the dragonet within.

"No," Luke said. "There will be no sacrificing." Nothing beyond another dose of dragon's blood. But one thing at a time. He turned his attention to William. "Better for you not to know too many details. There are crates in the cellar."

The boy nodded and gently pushed at Zia's head until—with a sigh—she pulled away. He stood.

"Take whatever you want from the great hall," Natalia dropped her hands onto William's shoulders and steered him toward the door. "But remember to focus on that which you'll need to open a studio." She ruffled his hair. "No stealing any crossbows."

"Aww." The young man flashed her an unrepentant grin.

"Off with you. Don't worry about Aileen. I'll speak with her and ensure she agrees to our plan. Soon." She closed the door behind William, turned about and fell backward against it. Exhaustion pulled at her features. "Care to share your brilliant plan?"

"There's an abandoned boat in the weeds. A simple motor with a propeller. A bit rusty, but—"

"You want to head up the river, toward the Trossachs?" She pushed off the door, frowning. Crossed the room to sit beside him upon the bench. "They'll follow us, attack us en route. Even if Zia donates more of her blood, not only are you sick—and looking worse by the moment—this plan of yours will carry us far beyond any laboratories." She lifted his hand, brushing her thumb over his knuckles. "Any hope for a cure..."

Gone.

Zia let out a low chirr, then stood and stretched her wings, pacing in circles about the room. Something was wrong. His eyes darted to the windows, searching the dark night outside. Nothing. He listened, but could hear nothing. William would be deep in the cellars, gathering packing materials. Was that what the dragon sensed?

"How long since she last ate?" Hunger, another possibility. "She's not left that nest unguarded since I've arrived."

"And rarely before that." Natalia stood and headed back toward the door. "Perhaps she simply needs to go out. Zia?"

But the dragon ignored her, continuing to pace the flagstones, lifting her nose and flicking her tongue.

Sampling the environment as if searching out something amiss. Then Zia stopped, motionless but for the flicking of her forked-tongue. Sensing something, she darted forward, stopping before Luke's makeshift nest.

"Zia, no!" Natalia dove for the rejected egg at the same time Luke leapt to his feet, trying to ignore the slight tilting of the room as he too lunged forward.

But they were both too late. Zia already gripped it between her jaws. With the flick of her head, she threw it aside.

Crunch.

With an anguished cry, Natalia scooped the broken egg from the floor into her hands. Within the fragments of shell curled a tiny dragonet, a significant yolk sac still attached. She lay still, unmoving. There was no first breath of atmospheric air. No rise and fall of the ribcage. Not so much as a twitch of her toe. Far too young, far too small to have had any hope of survival.

"I'm sorry." Luke lifted the tiny creature free from the shell, checking and rechecking to be certain there was nothing to be done.

Natalia looked up at him, tears brimming in her eyes. "Is she—"

He shook his head. "Dead." But only recently. "Zia sensed something. Remember, this dragonet wasn't developing at the same pace as the others, as the viable ones."

"Insufficient heat?" Guilt threaded through her voice.

Tempting to lie by way of comfort, but Natalia wouldn't appreciate such an instinct. "Possibly," he admitted. "But there could have been any number of causes. Things go wrong in development all the time."

Silent, they stood for a long moment, watching as Zia resumed her sentinel position, guarding her three remaining eggs.

Then Natalia gasped.

"Luke." He looked up to see her staring down at egg remnants—fluids, blood vessels and membranes—in her hands. Not in horror, but in wonder. "Stem cells. If the dragonet died recently—and not due to disease or congenital defect, then I'm holding stem cells. This is a chance to turn misfortune and death into something good. This means we don't need to wait for the other dragonets to hatch. If there are viable stem cells here, I can collect them." She spun on her heel and strode to her workbench.

Quietly, he followed her, laying the tiny dragonet upon a stretch of cotton batting. Perhaps they could spare a few moments for a quiet burial before they departed. He touched her arm. "The others leave at dawn. If we're to have any hope of evading Ivanov and Kravchuk, we need to depart at the same hour. That's less than twelve hours to arrange our escape. That can't possibly be long enough." All laboratory procedures seemed to require long, drawn out protocols with carefully timed steps. "If I've any hope of accompanying you, wouldn't dragon's blood be the better approach?"

"There's time," she insisted, fetching a beaker from a shelf filled with glassware. Natalia carefully placed the egg remnants inside, then turned to the shelves, lifting down bottles of various reagents. An intense fire lit her eyes. "And if this works, it will work fast. Your fever, your liver... any minor complaint will be remedied before the sun rises."

"That fast?" His heart leapt beneath his ribs. Unbelievable. Yet he couldn't help but hope...

"I need three hours." Keeping her eyes on her task, she pipetted a clear liquid into the beaker, rinsing the inside surface of the shells, collecting any and all tissues from their surfaces. "To collect all the cells, then to isolate the amniotic stem cells." She swirled the contents of the beaker. "These cells—according to Papa's notes—are highly mitotic, undifferentiated and immunoprivileged. Chances are the stem cells will colonize and proliferate not just inside your liver, but within additional tissue, in locations we are not specifically targeting. Because there will only be a tiny number of them, I suggest you take the anti-rejection medication to guard against any xenogenic immune response."

Wonder at her brilliant mind filled him, overflowing. But he didn't follow. "Perhaps in simpler words?"

She glanced up at him. "I'm going to collect the cells and inject them into your liver. They might all die, but with luck, they'll grow and spread inside of you. The medication will help keep your body from rejecting them, even though the temporary suppression of your immune system is likely to spike your fever even further. As to the stem cells, I can't predict the side effects, but they're likely to be... interesting." Her wobbly smile wasn't reassuring. "I doubt you'll acquire the ability to breathe fire, but..."

He was to become a human Petri dish. Wonderful.

But this might be his only chance to attempt such a stem cell treatment. If his liver managed to repair itself, he could live with a few patches of scales upon his skin so long as it meant he could spend his life with her.

"Here." Natalia paused, rummaged in a drawer, tossing one item after another aside—a broken pocket watch, a small radial clamp and a snap tinder lighter—before she pulled out a packet of pills and shook one free. "Take this. It's a sulfated purine derivative, a bit hard on the liver and, given the infection festering inside your wound, I don't want to risk more than one dose to suppress the immune system while the stem cells colonize the tissue."

Risk. Everything was happening so fast. He had two choices. Decline and pray his body fought off the bacteria infecting his arm. Or accept the risk, take a leap of faith, and hope for a miracle. What real choice was there? He took the pill from her and washed it down with a gulp of cold tea.

He had little to lose and everything to gain.

CHAPTER NINE

Rubbing her aching neck and rolling her shoulders, Natalia straightened, triumphant. She let the lightness in her chest bubble upward into a broad smile. Papa would be so proud. The isolated, pluripotent dragon stem cells now floated in a swirl of specially-formulated liquid media—one containing vitamins, inorganic salts, amino acids and glucose—recovering from several rounds of fractionation, digestive enzyme assaults, and differential density spins in the fuge. The cells needed a few minutes to rest—according to her father's notations—but time ran short. A glance at her timepiece informed her that if they were to abandon Castle Kinlarig at dawn, they would need to attempt this most basic of stem cell transplants within the next hour.

Particularly as Luke's infected wound grew more worrisome. Neither the application of more ethyl alcohol nor an additional treatment of dragon's blood—both performed hastily while cells spun—had done much to reduce the putrid-smelling pus that oozed from the cut or slow the spread of the red streaks.

The excitement of realizing the dragon eggs could hold the cure for Luke's illness had all but vaporized when Ivanov and Dimitri had landed in her courtyard with their demands. Not enough time was left to slowly work her way through her father's instructions, checking and double-checking each step. Instead she was rushed, harried and increasingly distressed by thoughts of what might happen should this impromptu treatment fail.

Her smile faltered. What if her best wasn't good enough? If this attempt failed, there would be no second chance. There wasn't time, not even if she were willing to sacrifice a dragonet. Luke might well die. She and Zia would be hauled back to Russia along with the dragon eggs where all would suffer untold torments. Worry gnawed at the inside of her stomach and began to crawl its way upward to lodge beneath her heart. She didn't want to ever be parted from Luke again. Not for *any* reason.

Zia was back to guarding her remaining three eggs and barely shifted as Natalia set about gathering supplies. After placing the vial containing the precious cells upon a metal tray alongside a syringe and needle of intimidating size, she made her way into the great hall where, as she'd worked, spates of crashing and banging had echoed. She stepped into the room, taking in the scene before her.

Luke—feverish—sat upon a chair, ignoring pain and discomfort to keep an eye on castle activity when he ought to be in bed, resting. He gave her a faint smile, tipping his head toward William's industriousness. Hay was strewn across the floor as the young man worked to pack swords and armor into crates. At her approach, he paused at his task.

"Impressive progress," she said. An entire wall was bare.

"This is the last crate," William said. "The steam wagon is fixed and loaded, and I've filled the coal hopper. Mr. Dryden and I," he cleared his throat, "took care of the body."

"He means," Luke interjected, "that we dragged Rathail's hunter to the river and gave him the send-off he deserved."

"So we did." A corner of William's mouth twitched, but he shifted on his feet. "If you can convince Aileen to depart, we could leave at first light. I poked my head into the kitchens to let them know of our plans, but she was weeping still, and I'm not certain she heard my words through her tears. McKay is at an utter loss."

"I'll speak with them." Internally, she cringed. Coping with an emotional Aileen would be trying. She would want to shake sense into her—but would need to fight the urge. Possibly Aileen's teeth would rattle loose first.

"It's late. Mr. Dryden is ill. Head home, gather your things and snatch a few hours rest." Surely Aileen could be made to see reason by dawn?

William hammered a few more nails, then heaved a crate onto his shoulder, calling a brief, "Good night."

Alone, she sank onto a chair beside Luke, tipping her weary head onto his shoulder, drawing strength from his presence even as her hand sought out his wrist, taking measure of his pulse. Weak and thready. It grew more worrisome every time she checked. The only way to save him now was to charge bravely ahead.

"Is it time?" he asked. "Shall we adjourn to your laboratory?" Impossible to tell if that was anticipation or worry in his voice. Probably both.

How many times had they sat here together at the high table of the great hall, deeply engrossed in conversation, or battled each other in the expanse of this space when the weather did not permit them to spar in the courtyard? Always careful to keep any physical contact fleeting, constantly aware of the forbidden attraction that simmered between them.

She'd been a married woman, her continued presence in this country dependent upon the goodwill of her absent husband and the funds provided to her by the very institution that employed Luke. *Lady* Kinlarig could not afford to tarnish her reputation. It didn't matter that the lord of the castle traipsed about with an actress upon each of his arms, entertaining his women with funds meant to delve into the organic chemistry of dragon venom in search of medical applications. Her appeals to the Department of Cryptozoology fell on deaf ears. She was to rise above it. To work without complaint while she waited for her laird to return home, to declare his intent to sire an heir.

And that was exactly what she would have done, had they not sent one Mr. Luke Dryden. He was back. They were both free. To be able to lean against Luke without a guilty conscious was a priceless luxury. But one she wouldn't be able to enjoy for long if his arm did not heal, his liver failed or—a more immediately relevant possibility—if Dimitri and Ivanov ran him through with a blade. A decided possibility should they attempt to run. Outside the relative safety of the castle, the Russians held the air advantage and, as sick as he was, Luke would be easy prey. Even at full strength, the odds would be against them. She could fret all she wished, but if they did not risk the stem cell treatment, a dark cloud hung over their future. Time to chase after everything she'd dreamed of: a loving husband and children. Zia free and happy surrounded by her own brood.

"Soon. We've a moment. The cells are resting. Recovering from the shock they've been put through." Threading her fingers between his, she squeezed his rough, calloused and all-too warm hand. "With all that's happened, do you not regret the day you learned dragons are real?"

"Not in the slightest." Luke dropped a kiss on top of her hair, and she smiled. It had been far too long since she'd felt cherished. "Father tried for years to discourage my dreams of working with extraordinary creatures. Banking, he insisted, was the path to happiness and security. But his plans for his son were a lost cause from the first moment I watched a pteryform soar overhead and announced I would become a—"

"Zookeeper." She'd heard the story long ago. Smiling, she tipped her face upward and basked in the warmth of his passion.

"Dragonkeeper has an even better ring to it." He tucked a loose strand of her hair behind her ear and trailed the backs of his fingers over the edge of her jaw. A shiver ran across her skin. "I fell in love with you the day we met." His voice was a whispered confession, but as she leaned forward and closed her eyes, his hand fell away. Disappointed, her eyes fluttered open. "When this is over, Natalia, you could attend a Season in London. Dissolute gentlemen are in the habit of stalking young heiresses. Perhaps you might turn the game on its head and snag yourself a wealthy industrialist, one who could maintain this castle and support your research."

Her lips flattened into a hard line. A declaration of love followed by a suggestion she wed another? "Absolutely not." She stood and crossed her arms, tucking her balled fists beneath her arms. Slapping a sick man wasn't an option. But perhaps after she cured him...

"Relying on government funds is always an uncertain existence."

"As is relying on a man." She threw him a sideways glare. Particularly ones who took themselves off to hunt dragon eggs in the Ural Mountains. She kept those words to herself. He'd made no promises to her. How could he, married as she was?

Was. Widows had certain freedoms in this country. Perhaps she was a fool to dream of marrying again? She drew in a steadying breath.

"This corner of Scotland is lovely," she continued. "But I've no intention of continuing to molder away within the walls of this damp castle. I've begun negotiations with a distant Kinross cousin. If he cannot or will not offer a fair price, I intend to sell it to the highest bidder. The townhouse in Edinburgh should be more than sufficient for my needs." How she would manage Zia and her dragonets if there was no safe haven for them in the Trossachs was beyond her, but she'd cope with that problem later.

"I'm sorry." Luke winced. "But it needed to be said."

She disagreed. But she was done contemplating any future until their immediate obstacles were behind them. Uncurling her fingers, she held out a hand to Luke. From the bilious look upon his face, the anti-rejection medication was working at full strength. "Come. If you're still willing, it's time to perform the transplant."

"I've everything to gain, and nothing to lose." He looked up, the pale shade of his face highlighting the dark shadows beneath his cheekbones, but he grasped her hand. "However awful the cure, it can't be worse than the disease."

"Careful." Lips twisting, she pulled him upright. "You might yet regret your words. I'm a chemist, not a cell biologist, and attempting to follow a recipe for the first time. This might not work. But if it does, dragon stem cells are extremely aggressive. The effects, if they occur, are rapid and potent." She swallowed hard—willing her voice not to tremble—and finished. "We'll know in a matter of hours if I've succeeded in isolating them—if there's hope for a cure."

She wished she were as confident of success as she pretended to be, but any direct experience with dragon stem cells was limited to being the patient, not the physician. A memory of misery. Lying motionless in a bed. Tears flowing from the corners of her eyes. Every breath a struggle as death circled in the dark shadows overhead, waiting for an opportunity to sink its claws deep.

Luke's situation was not so dire, but the regenerative effects were likely to be unpleasant. No, that was putting it too mildly. Painful? Pure agony? Save for a necessary conversation with Aileen, she would stay by his side and attempt to ease his torment.

"Aggressive?" A look of worry crossed Luke's face. "Tell me, what was it like for you?"

Natalia was the first—and to her knowledge, only—human to ever undergo a dragon stem cell transplant and had never shared her story. Not a single living soul had any idea what she'd undergone.

While Dimitri had gloated and basked in the limelight of retrieving dragon eggs from the surrounding mountains in time for all to witness the hatchlings emerge, Papa had quietly collected the egg shell fragments. Busy shaking hands and rubbing shoulders with his superiors in a quest to elevate his position within the Ural Zavód, Dimitri hadn't noticed his mentor silently cultivating a cell type never before documented. Only when her father's absence from the laboratory was noted, did Dimitri think to wonder what had become of his betrothed.

Not that he took the trouble to visit, bastard that he was.

She swallowed. "I was hazy and nauseous—an effect of the anti-rejection medication—when my father arrived at my beside."

Luke nodded, urging her on with hope in his eyes. Hope she was about to pierce with a sharp lance.

"Numb from the neck down, I felt nothing as he injected small colonies of stem cells alongside the fractured vertebrae of my neck. Not a single twinge, not even when the needle punctured the membranes protecting my spinal cord as he inserted a number of stem cells directly into my cerebral spinal fluid." Closing her eyes, she forced the memory past her lips. Her body started to shake at the effort of voicing the memory. "An hour, maybe two, passed. Then there was a sudden burning sensation, a jolt as if an electric current raced down my back. Pain and pressure enveloped me as the stem cells invaded and repaired every bit of damaged tissue." They'd ripped down her spine, crawled over her nerve cord, dividing with unrelenting purpose. Locked in a nightmare, she'd felt every single cell as it crept about, ripping out damaged tissue to assemble something new. "I thought I was going to die."

He squeezed her hand. "But…"

"By morning scales were breaking through the skin of my back and neck." Building their keratin scaffolds with shocking speed. "The itch at the base of my neck, along the length of my spine, was almost unbearable. Papa nearly fell off his chair when I suddenly sat up and reached behind to scratch at a cluster of scales." No one had expected the transplant to work at all, let alone so quickly. "In less than twenty-four hours, I could walk again. All pain had vanished."

Undiluted awe lit Luke's eyes from within. "Amazing."

"It was." But with success came anguish. Bitterness surfaced. "It was also the end of my time in Russia. Dimitri turned in my father, his own mentor."

While her father sat by her bedside, Dimitri had searched the laboratory, collecting the few random scribbles Papa had left behind upon forgotten scraps of paper. The evidence was thin, but accusations and demands were made. Thinly veiled threats. Papa was to share the details of his experiment with his superiors— of which Dimitri now numbered—immediately, else he would be arrested, his daughter remanded into custody for observation.

Unthinkable. Dragon stem cells were a potent remedy and—in the wrong hands—too easily abused. Yet today—if all went well—she would set wrongs to right and give them all a chance at a brighter future.

"That bastard," Luke hissed. He reached for her, wrapping his arms about her.

With her recovered ability to walk, there really was no other choice but to flee. In a final act of treason, Papa had stolen the dragonets—Zia and Yuri—from the laboratory and... "We ran. The train was pulling away from the station. But Papa, he wasn't fast enough." *Go!* he'd yelled, pushing her in front of him, out of the way. Blocking her body with his own. "The guards caught sight of him." Her voice faltered. "Shot him where he stood." She brushed away a tear that ran down her cheek. The bullet had dropped him to the cinders beside the track. He'd sacrificed himself to save her.

Weeping, she'd clutched Zia and Yuri to her chest. Numb, she'd followed the plan. West to Scotland. To Edinburgh. To the Department of Cryptozoology. Throwing herself on their mercy.

"I'm so sorry." Luke kissed her forehead and, for a moment, she allowed herself to savor the warm, comforting circle of his arms. But only for a moment. She would not allow another man she loved to fall on her behalf. Not while it was within her power to prevent it. The very thought of failure made her heart twist within her chest.

Shoving away memories of the past, she focused upon what must be done in the here and now. She cleared her throat and pulled back. "I'll collect the cells. Make yourself comfortable in my bed." A touch of heat rose to her cheeks. "If this works, you're going to feel much worse before you feel any improvements."

"It will work," he said with a confidence she didn't at all feel, tugging her back against his chest to press a fierce and fevered kiss to her lips, reminding her of other things worth fighting for. "Perhaps even fast enough for us to explore any interesting side effects that might result."

CHAPTER TEN

Luke stripped off his waistcoat and shirt, pulled off his boots and then stretched out upon the bed. Holding his pocket watch in his hand, he noted the hour. Half past nine o'clock in the evening. Nine hours until sunrise. What if these stem cells didn't work? Or didn't work fast enough? But if they did...

Despite the fever heating his skin, entertaining such thoughts already had him in a state of half-arousal. He wanted nothing more than to free the weight of her breasts from that corset that teased his eyes with every glance he'd dared allow to skim its intimately-contoured leather surface, to slip his hands beneath the loose gathers of her tunic while nibbling at the curve of her neck, to...

He tugged a blanket to his waist, hiding his interest. But if the procedure worked, he had every intention of dragging her back into his arms and into this very bed. He'd thought himself reconciled to a brief affair—until she'd announced her intention to sell the castle, refusing to even consider marrying a wealthy gentleman to save this ancient pile of rocks. Pure relief had swept over him, and he'd begun to wonder if perhaps he could convince her to marry a certain dragonkeeper? Would she be willing to exchange the title of Lady Kinlarig for the simpler one of Mrs. Dryden?

"Ready?" Steel and glass rattled upon a metal tray, yanking him out of his thoughts as Natalia crossed the room to his side.

Sitting up, he swallowed at the sight of the large bore needle screwed into the barrel of a syringe that held a cloudy, pinkish-orange fluid. Beside it rested a bottle of ethyl alcohol and cotton lint. "That's it? A single injection?" But then what had he expected from mere shell fragments?

"I was only able to collect a few thousand or so cells." She set the tray on the bedside table and flashed him a tense smile that did nothing to settle his nerves. Was he worried? Of course. But without risk there was no reward. "Without an incubator or appropriate growth media to culture the cells—to allow them to replicate— we've no choice but to make do."

Tugging a thick textbook from beneath her arm, she placed it between them upon the mattress and began flipping through the pages, stopping at a diagram of the liver. "Our next step is to determine aim. Any and all input as to where I should send these cells is encouraged."

A wave of apprehension rolled over him, collapsing all lingering thoughts of bed sport. A chemist masquerading as a biologist who was in turn playing doctor. Between the two of them, he was the one with more in-depth anatomical knowledge. But of rare and unusual animals. Still, human anatomy couldn't be that different, could it?

Her finger landed on the image. "Here?" She sounded doubtful. "If I angle the needle upward and into the liver from beneath the right side of the rib cage?"

He bent over the text, scanned the image and the words inscribed beside it, then shrugged. "The largest lobe does present a broad target." A more refined target—such as the hepatic portal vein—would require abdominal surgery. *That* wasn't happening.

"Agreed. The largest lobe it is."

Though their words were bold and confident, threading through their voices was the slightest of tremors.

Eyeballing the location of the human liver beneath the rib cage on the textbook's page—and carefully accounting for left-right—he moved a finger alongside the lower edge of his right ribcage to the side of his sternum, attempting to pinpoint the same location to which she pointed. The cure for his condition felt as if it had been reduced to a game of darts played in a public house. Better than a game of chance, but not by much.

He pushed inward, then hissed between clenched teeth as a deep, gnawing ache radiated outward from his fingertip sending tendrils of pain wrapping around his back.

"Luke?" Her face contorted with worry.

"Found a likely spot," he gasped. And fell back onto the pillows, careful to keep his fingertip firmly in place. "Aim here. I'm ready." He'd been sick for so long, he wasn't certain he knew what healthy felt like anymore.

She touched the lint to the lip of the glass bottle, soaking the fibers with alcohol. "If you'll move your finger." He lifted his hand, and there was a flash of wet, then cold as the ethyl alcohol touched his skin and evaporated. "Brace yourself." Lifting the syringe, she smiled, though her body was tense with the effort. "Take a deep breath, hold it, and—whatever you do—don't move."

His heart raced. They'd reached the point of no return. He dragged in a deep breath, gritted his teeth and—though every instinct screamed at him to squeeze his eyes shut—focused upon the bed hangings that stretched above while holding every muscle in his body rigid.

A sharp pain bit into the skin beneath his rib cage and radiated outward into his right shoulder. A dull sensation of pressure followed as she depressed the plunger. Then a moment later—for good or ill—it was done.

He exhaled as Natalia pressed a soft piece of lint against the injection site and held it there. For several long minutes—measured only by the thudding of his heart—in which he hardly dared move, their eyes locked.

Concern wrinkled her brow. "Do you feel anything?"

The continued aching throb of the infected cut on his arm, but otherwise... "Nothing—" His eyebrows drew together, and he pressed his palm beneath his ribcage, where an odd, subtle pressure built. "It feels... warm?"

"A good sign." She lifted away the lint. A tiny pinprick was the only outward indication that anything unusual had transpired. Pulling the blanket over his bare chest, Natalia stood. "Rest. Sleep if you can. I hate to leave you, but I need to speak with Aileen. Before she takes it into her mind to act rashly. Again."

"Go. She shouldn't stay here." Men—for more would follow—seeking a dragon wouldn't hesitate to stoop to low tactics. A rush of heat flooded his heart. Were the stem cells already on the move? The textbook had shown a direct connection between the liver and the heart. Possible then. He'd wonder about it more. Later. When his mind wasn't drifting. He felt so very tired...

"Luke?" Concern colored her voice.

"I'm fine. Just sleepy." He forced himself to finish. "Find out everything she told Ivanov. If he sent reports to anyone but Kravchuk."

"Of course." She smoothed his brow. "Now sleep. I'll be right back."

He caught her hand and pressed a kiss to her palm, then let her go. The sooner she spoke with Aileen, the sooner she would return. As his eyelids grew heavy, he caught a final flash of color. His love wrapping a scarf about her neck, concealing her secret. From everyone but him.

A heavy weight pressed down upon him, sinking him ever deeper into the feather mattress. He listened to the faint footfalls of Natalia's exit as sleep caught at him, pulling him into blessed oblivion.

A moment later, an odd crawling sensation overtook his innards.

His eyes snapped open. *So soon?* Anxiety pressed down on his chest. "Natalia?"

~~~

The kitchens—with its massive fireplace, enormous cast iron range, and line of steam servants all standing at attention and collecting cobwebs—was meant to be a busy, bustling and warm room. The heart of the castle. Instead, it was reduced to a drafty, cold space. Its only occupants sat, hunched and motionless, at the long, scarred worktable while the ever-present cabbage soup simmered over a small coal fire burning in the range.

Aileen lifted her head from her hands to glance at Natalia with a tear-stained face, before turning her back.

"Lady Kinlarig!" McKay lurched to his feet when Natalia stepped into the room. "I'm so sorry. My granddaughter's actions are shameful. A betrayal of your trust—"

She held up a hand. "I'll speak with her directly in a moment." McKay's face collapsed, but he held his tongue. "You've heard the noise, seen William dashing about the castle?"

"Indeed." McKay cleared his throat. "My deepest apologies for allowing the lad into our household. He harbors the misconception that he has been granted permission to run off with a large portion of the weapons collection. I attempted to bring the situation to your attention, but Mr. Dryden prevented me from speaking to you, claiming pressing concerns in the laboratory."

"Is that so?" Luke, her very own guard. Natalia suppressed a smile. It had been a long time since anyone had looked out for her.

"It is." McKay scowled as he worked to straighten his spine. "Over my objections, William has been hard at work all evening loading the steam wagon. Would you believe he had the temerity to *order* us to pack our bags, to *inform* us that we are to evacuate to the Edinburgh townhouse?" He sniffed. "A Kinross has never abandoned his lands, and a McKay has always stood by his side."

His.

Any plans the last laird might have had for an heir had been cut short before he'd attempted to resume relations with his long-abandoned wife. Had he treated Zia with respect and not as an investment to be sold in times of need, Natalia might well have cooperated with his desire to sire a child. After all, divorce had not been an option—not when Zia was legally recognized as his property, and Natalia had always longed for a family.

Instead, the fool had baited a dragon. Without such basic common sense, it was fortunate, perhaps, that he had sired no children.

As it stood *she* was the last Kinross, a tenuous and nominal designation only. But to ensure his cooperation and move McKay and his granddaughter out of harm's way, she would embrace her status as Lady Kinlarig. For the sake of the youngest McKay who now found herself in a fraught situation.

Not to mention the state of household funds, a pressing concern. Selling the castle and its contents would—at the very least—staunch the rate at which their finances deteriorated. It would buy all of them time to make alternative plans for their futures.

"The Laird of Kinlarig's death has led to a dispute over the legal definition of moveable property, in particular, livestock," Natalia began. "The men who besiege our castle will not cease their attempts to exert their presumed authority. Until certain matters are settled, we will be more comfortable adjourning to the townhome." Where her husband had kept mistresses, whisky and aether knew what else. She hoped his paramours hadn't carried off everything saleable, but odds were faint. "I'm counting on your wisdom and experience to help restore the family's good name. That task begins in Edinburgh."

That brought McKay's chin up. "If we must."

"We must." She injected as much authority as she could manage into her voice. "The townhome will no doubt require a firm hand and extensive reorganization. William has loaded the steam wagon and filled its fire box. He leaves at dawn. Will you please accompany him?"

McKay's eyes glittered, perhaps at the thought of once again having an extensive staff to do his every bidding.

"I will, but..." His gaze drifted to Aileen who sat quietly at the table, refusing to look in their direction.

There was one more McKay to convince, and for that Natalia required a few private moments.

"Today's... excitement has overtired Mr. Dryden and dragged him to bed, but I hope his condition will soon turn a corner." She tapped the iron shoulder of the motionless steam cook. "Given we are to leave Castle Kinlarig, perhaps we might indulge, use our remaining supplies—coal, flour, sugar—to prepare a substantial breakfast? This steambot, I seem to recall, was most excellent at baking."

"I'll see to it, my lady," McKay said, then busied himself with the task of firing up the steam cook.

Exhausted by the events of the day, she dropped onto the bench beside Aileen. Perhaps, for the first time in over three years of forced coexistence, they might manage to see eye to eye.

"Michael—Misha Ivanov—is a bastard and not worth your tears." Natalia unhooked the sack of coins from her belt and held it out. "Refusing his money accomplishes nothing save to make you poorer."

Aileen caught up the heavy pouch, then turned red-rimmed eyes to meet Natalia's gaze. "You can't possibly wish me to work in your city townhome, not with me in," Aileen flapped a hand at her waistline, "in such a situation."

McKay sucked in a shocked breath of air. He turned, trundling to the far side of the kitchen to riffle through an assortment of recipe punch cards.

Three years of accumulated resentments towered between her and Aileen and was not an easy wall to scale. Yet, for the sake of the child's future and McKay's pride, she'd see it surmounted. "There's no need for us to work at cross purposes. Nor must we be friends to form an alliance. Shall we set aside all personal differences and speak plainly?"

For a long moment Aileen said nothing, and Natalia's hope began to flag. Perhaps bitterness ran too deep?

"How do you propose I remedy my situation?" Aileen asked, her eyes narrow.

"Take a new name," Natalia said. "Attach the title missus before it. As our families dwindle, so too do those who can prove that you are not, in fact, a young widow. Particularly in the city."

Aileen looked doubtful. Such was not a traditional stance here in Britain where housekeepers were generally unmarried and childless. "You would let me continue as a housekeeper, after..."

"If you wish to keep the child? Yes." She dropped her voice. "Perhaps I ought to abandon you, but I feel a certain responsibility, given my presence at Castle Kinlarig precipitated our current situation." She smoothed her hand over the scarf at her neck. "Dragons. Unwelcome men misrepresenting themselves while stalking our grounds before dropping into our courtyard astride pteryformes."

Aileen's face twisted. "Mr. Dryden called him Misha?"

"Misha Ivanov. His Russian name. Michael is an anglicized form. He was sent here to collect information about the dragon, about my work."

"And found seduction the path of least resistance." Aileen slumped under the weight of the inescapable truth. Her lover was a married man. A hard-hearted mercenary. A foreigner not welcome on British soil. They had no future.

The time for difficult questions had arrived. "I need to know how much and exactly what you told him."

"Michael—*Misha*—wished to know about the town rumors that the castle housed a flying reptile. I told him you had a pet lizard. Whatever you call that creature's method of flapping about the halls, it's certainly not *flying*."

True.

"It wasn't until after we..." Aileen cleared her throat. "He asked if I was your laboratory assistant and was disappointed when I told him I wanted nothing to do with chemistry or poisons. But he started pressing for more information. That's when I knew he had no interest in textile mills. I confronted him. He told me it was a matter of British security." She lowered her eyes, her voice petulant. "I didn't want to go anywhere near that awful beast, or step into that foul-smelling laboratory of yours, but by then I had begun to suspect..." Her hand fell upon her abdomen. "I'm sorry. I couldn't risk him leaving me."

"That's why you've been trying to befriend Zia." Irritation zinged through her, tempered by sympathy for the situation Aileen had found herself in.

Aileen nodded. "He gave me a yellow rock earlier, promised no dragon could resist such a treat. He told me as soon as he could confirm you weren't a threat, we could marry and move to Edinburgh." A fresh tear trickled down her cheek, and she slapped it away. "I was a fool. He's a spy, but not one of ours."

If only she and Aileen had been on speaking terms, if only Natalia had insisted upon meeting her suitor, they might have nipped their situation in the bud. But there was nothing to do save keep a keen eye so that they might avoid such a situation in the future should Russia ever show interest in her again. Assuming they survived *this* encounter.

"So will you go?" Natalia asked. "To the Edinburgh townhome?"

"I don't see how," Aileen stated. "Michael and that other man will never let *you* pass. We won't reach Stirling, let alone Edinburgh. Not so long as they have," she flapped a hand, "those beasts to fly upon. They will swoop down, confiscate your dragon and lead you away in chains." She slanted a questioning glance at Natalia, at the scarf about her neck. "What about your *skin disease* interests them so?"

Everything. "I have no idea." She needed to return to Luke's bedside. If the transplant had been successful, the dragon stem cells would begin their work soon, and he ought not be left alone. "I won't be traveling to Edinburgh. Not yet. Mr. Dryden and I have other arrangements for Zia."

Aileen's lips twisted. "More details I shouldn't know?"

"For your own safety. For mine." And because Natalia didn't quite trust her. "You can't share what you don't know." She would ask once more. A final attempt to save Aileen from herself. "Will you go?"

"I'll go," she said, but grudgingly. "I can't promise I'll stay, not forever, but I'll help my grandfather set the house to rights."

"Good enough." Standing, Natalia raised her voice, inviting McKay—who now had the steam cook huffing and puffing—back into the conversation. "Pteryformes are nocturnal, that is why you must leave at dawn. The steam wagon will travel the most obvious route to Edinburgh, your destination and intentions not at all a mystery. Expect Ivanov and Kravchuk to track you as dusk falls, perhaps sooner. Hide nothing. Do what you must to keep yourselves safe. With luck, Mr. Dryden, Zia and I will be well away."

McKay, realizing that the two women had finally come to terms, unbent, turned and stopped feigning deafness. He held up a punch card. "I've a likely recipe for cream cakes."

In an unprecedented move, Aileen threw her arms about Natalia, giving her a brief, but fierce hug before hopping away, color high upon her cheeks. "Thank you. I'll bring a tea tray up?"

Her housekeeper—no matter their newly reconciled state—couldn't be allowed to learn of the dragon eggs. If questioned—and she would be—news of them would be sent home to Russia, redoubling efforts to track them. A lost dragon was one thing. Rumors of an improbable cure would fade to myth. But whispers about a clutch of eggs would invite speculation about a breeding colony of dragons in the mountains of Scotland, and her former countrymen would never cease their hunt.

"What, brave the dragon who nips at your ankles?" She shook her head, a smile tugging at her lips as she filled a large pitcher with cool water for Luke. "No need. Leave it outside the laboratory door." A door which would be locked. "Mr. Dryden and I have our own preparations to make."

A touch of mischief crossed Aileen's face, and she winked. "Ones I'm better off not knowing about?"

She certainly hoped so. It was Natalia's turn to blush.

CHAPTER ELEVEN

Luke clutched at the bedding. A thousand clawed kraken tentacles gripped his intestines. Spiders with needle-like legs crawled through his veins and arteries. Fire ants ran beneath his skin turning every square inch of his flesh to ash.

Thud. A heavy weight landed on his chest, forcing all but his last breath from his lungs. *Flick.* A lash of a damp tongue. *Swish.* A rough tail skittering across bed sheets.

He pried open scalded eyelids and found himself staring into Zia's golden eyes. The dragon had somehow managed to flutter-hop onto the bed, onto his chest. Concerned enough to leave her eggs in order to investigate disturbing sounds from the above bedchamber. She flicked her tongue out to touch his nose, then she nudged her smooth snout beneath one hand and tossed it in the air, slipping beneath to ensure his palm fell upon her head. *Pet me.*

"Natalia?" he rasped.

Silence.

His legs were tangled in twists of bedclothes and every pillow had been tossed to the floor. He pushed at the dragon, panting at the effort of shifting her bulk. But Zia's weight was significant, and he couldn't breathe. Disappointed or disturbed, Zia moved to the bottom of the bed, pinning his feet beneath her stomach as he gasped for air.

Tap, tap, tap. The sound of boots on the stairs.

He turned his aching head. "Natalia?"

"Zia!" Natalia scolded as she stepped into the room. "Down."

With an irritated flapping of wings, the dragon departed, stomping noisily across the floor, before slinking back down the stairs, no doubt to oversee her unhatched eggs. But not before pausing to stare for a long moment at her mistress, as if to accuse her of abandoning her favorite man.

Luke was in complete agreement. "Need water," he whispered.

In a heartbeat, Natalia was by his side, holding a cool glass to his dry, cracked lips as he took in great gulps of water. "Aether, you're burning up."

"Thank you," he said as she set aside the cup to tuck pillows beneath his head. "These cells, I swear they've invaded the entirety of my body." He described the disturbing sensations coursing throughout him.

"We did inject them directly into a most highly perfused organ." She mopped his forehead with a damp cloth, though her presence alone was calming. "But these stem cells do seem most potent and intent."

"*Something* is happening," he said. "It feels as if I'm being turned inside out."

"I'm so sorry." She clasped his hand to her chest, staring down at him with worry etched into every feature. "I've spoken with Aileen. Everything is settled, and I'll not leave you again until this is over. Can you sleep?"

"Perhaps." The corner of his mouth hitched upward. "If a beautiful woman were to lay by my side and run her fingers soothingly through my hair."

Though she rolled her eyes, her fingers were already unbuckling the sword belt from her waist. With a clatter, the various items clipped to it fell to the ground. She dropped her sweet arse onto the mattress beside him and began to unlace her knee-high boots. *Thunk. Thunk.* She peeled away stockings, her scarf. And then she was climbing in beside him, though regrettably still dressed in trousers, tunic and corset.

When her soft curves finally rested against his side, and her arm draped over his waist, the various creatures that held his body in their grip were pacified, slowing—if not ceasing—their mad scramble to alter all they found amiss within him.

He closed his eyes, submitting to their repairs.

~~~

Luke's heated skin smoldered through the layers of clothing she wore, but whenever she moved away, he would begin to groan and writhe in his sleep, a slumber so deep she could not rouse him. And so she stayed, committed to keeping her arms wrapped about a veritable furnace, unwilling to disturb—however slightly—his healing process.

Time passed in a haze as she drifted in and out of a light sleep, waking to blot Luke's forehead, to hold yet another glass of water to his lips. He imbibed an impressive quantity of water as enzymatic cascades worked overtime, shredding away damaged tissues within his body before setting about the process of repairing and restructuring.

Eventually, exhaustion claimed her, and she fell into her own fevered dreams.

Dreams which became increasingly erotic until her eyes fluttered open. *Not a dream.*

Luke's hard body was pressed against her backside, and though his erection made his interest evident, it was his fingers that moved, working magic wherever they touched.

Already, he'd tugged loose the drawstring of her chemise and managed to unbuckle the top two fasteners of her leather corset. Not that she minded. Not at all. The slow slide of his rough skin over her puckered nipple sent a rush of warmth between her legs.

"Mmm," she hummed. She tipped her head backward against his shoulder and her braid tumbled free. *Someone* had been stealing hairpins while she slept. "Feeling better?"

"Much." He nipped her earlobe, his hot breath brushing across the curve of her neck. "The wound to my arm, healed. All pain, gone. But I still feel as if a fire is burning inside. Whatever transformations your cells have wrought, they've left me ravenous." He rolled her nipple between his fingers. "Any objection if I proceed to devour you?" His rough voice woke every last nerve.

"None," she gasped out, feeling wanton. "Though I'd rather be claimed." She twitched her hips backward to emphasize her point. "Fully. Completely."

A growl of approval tore from his throat, and his hand tightened on her breast, his fingers pinching her nipple and ripping a cry of pleasure from her throat.

Buckle by buckle, her corset fell open beneath his fingers. Gathering the material of her chemise in his fist, he yanked it upward, then spread the surface of his palm across the expanse of her bare stomach. The heat of his touch and the cool rush of air sent shivers running over her skin.

All the while, his lips kissed, bit, and then soothed the skin of her neck just below her ear, fanning the flames of desire yet higher. She squirmed in his embrace—her hands falling upon forearms that seemed to have muscles of braided wire—desperate to pull away, if only to rip the clothing from her body. But he held her tight against his stiff cock, all while slowly slipping his hand beneath the waistband of her trousers.

His fingertips spread her slick folds, resuming their earlier exploration of all that brought her pleasure. His hand slid deeper, pushing a finger into her tight channel, working her gently, until her hips began to jerk against his hand and a delicious pressure threatened to crest.

"No." She grabbed his wrist and pulled his hand away. "Not this way. I want you inside me." Buried deep while she reached for her pleasure.

Twisting, she stabbed her fingers into his thick hair, dragging his mouth to hers. Their tongues tangled, and she tasted the salt of his sweat and the heat of his desire. Fire licked over her skin.

He reared back. "Clothes. Off."

Her braid tumbled loose as she rose up on her knees, shrugging off her corset and pulling her chemise over her head. Luke growled in appreciation, his hands yanking the soft wool of her trousers down her hips. Then he lifted his gaze to hers.

"Your eyes." She clasped his face—rough with stubble—between her palms, staring. "They're not brown anymore—not entirely. There are flecks of gold streaking through them. They all but glow." *Glorious.*

Toppling her backward, he stripped away the last of her clothing, then loomed over her. "Has anything else changed?" He grinned as her gaze traveled over his naked glory.

"I hardly had the chance to look earlier," she protested. But, *aether*, he was magnificent. Impossible not to run her hands over the hard planes and angles of his chest, his strong shoulders, his bulging arms. Strong. Healthy. Vibrant. "Before that, no matter how badly I wished to touch you so, I was a married woman."

"Was." He flipped onto his back, ridding himself of his own clothing.

She gasped. At the magnificent view, of course, but also at the scattering of scales beneath the edge of his rib cage where the needle had pierced his flesh. She dropped a fingertip to them, brushing their surface. "Can you feel that?"

"I can." He glanced down, flexing the muscles of his abdomen. A delighted grin stretched his mouth. "What of my arm?"

Natalia unwound the bandage. Another clustering of scales traced an alluring path across his biceps. She leaned close, pressing soft kisses to them. *Thank aether.* The treatment had worked. Blinking back the tears that welled in her eyes, she lifted her gaze and stared into his blazing eyes. "Fully healed." And more evenly matched for the fight that was to come. She pushed the thought aside. First, a celebration.

"An amazing recovery." She sat up, her eyes drawn across the room to a lamp glowing upon the hearthside table. "Are you not the least bit—?" *Hungry.* But that word died on her lips. A tray rested there—one that must have been left outside the laboratory door—and it was empty, its contents devoured. "You ate everything?" It was clear she'd slept deeply, but how long?

Luke pulled her down on top of him. A rumbling laugh resonated in his chest. "Not everything."

~~~

Soft breasts and hard nipples slid over his chest as Natalia shifted away, reaching for her pocket watch. Her thigh grazed his rampant erection as she landed on her stomach, sending his mind into a blazing swirl of need. He rolled onto his side and smoothed a hand over the rise of her arse, a desperate attempt to rein himself in while she noted the time. With a fingertip, he traced a path across the scales clustered at the base of her spine. Green, with a flash of red fire.

"Four o'clock!" She dropped the pocket watch and glanced over her shoulder. Light danced in her eyes. A coy smile tipped the corner of her lips upward. "Like what you see?"

Aether, was that an invitation? He'd planned to hold back, to bring her to a climax before sinking into her sweet, wet sex. But this... Yes, *this* was what he wanted. To drive into her until she screamed his name.

Never before had he felt so alive, so strong. So filled with lust. But she was inexperienced... he shouldn't...

And yet...

He rose up and pulled her onto her knees, bent her forward until she fell upon her hands. He caught at her loose braid, giving it a sharp tug before dragging his hand down her back, across the scattering of scales that glinted in the moonlight. He stilled. "Do you want it like this? From behind?" *Rutting like animals?* He held his breath. Did the beasts inside them both pant for this, for a primitive coupling, an explosive release? His cock throbbed.

But he waited.

She dropped to her elbows. "Yes." Her voice was husky, her desire echoing his.

Still he held back. Nudging her knees apart, he slid a finger over her slick folds until she cried out, her voice a mixture of desperation and desire. His breath hitched with need. "Please."

Steadying her hips with one hand, he guided the broad head of his cock to her damp entrance. And sank into her tight channel a single inch. Easing out, he pushed forward again.

"Oh, Luke," she rasped. "Yes. More." She edged her knees farther apart, and he sank deeper, his hips pressing flush to hers.

His fingers dug into the soft, pliant flesh of her hips as his body blazed with lust. Impossible not to move. He drew back, and with one thrust, drove into her completely, into her tight, squeezing channel. "Natalia!" His breath was ragged.

Squirming, she arched her back and cried out, panting, groaning feverish words of encouragement that raced across his skin and burned in his ears as he plunged into her again and again, claiming her body with long, hard strokes.

His climax gathered at the base of his spine, drawing ever tighter. Buried deep, he paused. "No," he rasped, then slid free. He wanted to see her face, watch her eyes as they blazed with heat. For him.

"Luke!" A cry of frustration.

He pulled at her legs, dropping her onto her stomach, rolling her onto her back. Catching her mouth with his, he kissed her deeply.

She bit his lip, then wrenched her mouth away. "I need..."

Spreading her legs, she yanked him against her swollen center, and he slid inside. Her legs lifted, her ankles wrapped about his hips pulling him closer. Nails dug into the skin of his arse, and her pelvis tipped upward, encouraging his powerful, pistoning strokes.

He levered up onto his arms, shifting to thrust higher against her center. "Come!" he ordered.

Her sex clenched, clamping down on him. "Luke!" Her blue eyes blazed as she screamed his name.

Primitive satisfaction rushed through him, and he strained against her, grinding as he chased his own climax. With a roar, he drove into her with a final stroke and the world about him exploded. Lights flashed. Blood pounded. Air rushed from his chest. And his body collapsed. Just enough sense remained for him to tilt to the side, twisting as his shoulders hit the mattress. But he didn't let go. She came with him—hot, sweaty and limp—and landed upon his chest.

"Aether," he breathed, finally dragging enough oxygen into his lungs. He wrapped his arms tight about her.

"Magnificent." She dropped a tired head to his shoulder—her blonde braid a ragged tangle—and slipped a weary arm about his waist. "And still a few hours until dawn."

"Again?" A laugh rumbled in his chest, but already his cock twitched with interest.

With a fading voice, she whispered, "Soon." And drifted to sleep, snoring softly.

Luke stared at the bed canopy that arched above him. Health restored. Wrapped in the arms of the woman he loved. Safe. Everything he wanted within reach.

If he could but remove the one last remaining threat. Running would buy them time, but it wouldn't solve their problems, not permanently.

Ivanov and Kravchuk would have to be eliminated.

~~~

A murmur of muffled voices woke her. "Luke," she said, reaching out an arm. "We need to dress." But no one was there. The mattress beside her was cool.

Natalia snapped her eyes open and sat upright, clutching the sheet to her bare breasts as Luke—fully dressed—strolled back into the bedchamber, carrying a new tray laden with a teapot, cups and an abundance of baked treats. He moved with ease, without a hint of exhaustion or pain.

Not a dream. They'd done it. He was cured. Possibilities stretched before them, if only they could outrun, out-fight Ivanov and Kravchuk and their winged mounts. Excitement faded as a heaviness settled in her stomach. Another battle loomed, and she was so very tired of fighting. Of running. She wanted more time with Luke alone—here and now—but their best chance of surviving a confrontation with Dimitri and Ivanov was to draw them out unexpectedly, in daylight, when their pteryformes' vision was—at the very least—compromised.

Zia trundled along behind Luke, her tail swishing. Routine had been disrupted—on many levels—and she was keeping the newest human to enter the equation carefully in her line of sight.

Slivers of brilliant gold flashed in his eyes. "I wondered when you'd wake." He set down the tray and nodded at the window. A faint glimmer of light spilled through its thick glass. "The steam wagon is loaded. William, Aileen and McKay are shuttering windows and making last minute preparations. Our boat awaits, ready, save for its passengers. I took the liberty of coating a quiver's worth of arrows with your laboratory-refined venom to pair with your deadly aim and crossbow." He stopped beside the bed, his gaze caressing her exposed skin. Every nerve stood at attention, begging for more time. "About last night..."

She dropped the sheet. Grabbing his waistcoat with both hands, she pulled him down on top of her and kissed him, deeply, regretting every moment lost to slumber. The sword fastened to his hip pressed against her thigh as his hands fell upon her waist, sliding upward over her rib cage to cup the weight of her breasts.

But they were out of time.

Though he pulled away, a suggestive smile teased his lips, and an appreciative gaze slid over her nakedness, their thoughts both straying in the same carnal direction.

"Last night was amazing," she whispered, though words alone failed to convey how her world had tilted off axis, redefining and expanding the concept of bedroom sport. She needed *this* man in her life. Always and forever. No other would do.

Luke's expression sobered. "About last night, we forgot to..." He swallowed. "If there are consequences—"

Her lips parted in shock. Not horror. Any children of Luke's would be welcome, but she'd not wish to forcibly bind him to her that way. "We were careless."

"Swept up in the moment as we were, the fault lies with us both." He tipped up her chin. "If you conceive, we'll marry?"

Not at all the impassioned proposal a woman desired, but would she turn him away? Not a chance. She loved him. Tired of living a life apart, she had no use for an empty title or a drafty castle. But after her first cold, practical marriage, she wanted more than an offer of marriage that followed on the heels of a "mistake".

"This isn't the time for such a discussion." Natalia slid from the bed, pulling on her clothes, shoving her feet into her boots and lacing them tightly. She buckled her belt about her waist and slid daggers into place. "No." She held up a hand when he would press the matter. "We must focus, lest we not survive the day or, worse, find ourselves transported back to Russia."

His hand fell on the hilt of his rapier, and determination hardened his face. "Not a chance I'll allow that to happen."

She had no doubt he would do his best to prevent such an occurrence. But there was another weakness. "My father's notes." How she wished he could have met Luke, witnessed this triumph, recognized the potency of uncultured dragon stem cells. Lifting them from the table, she caught Luke's gaze, then turned to the fireplace. The yellowed pages were her last physical connection to her father. Her chest ached at the thought of destroying them, but she couldn't risk them falling into the wrong hands.

"Natalia, are you certain?" Worry filled his eyes. "This cure has been nothing short of miraculous."

"But in the wrong hands, the outcome could be monstrous. Cells harvested from a dragon's egg, from the developing embryo itself, might be even more potent. Conservation of a species will not even land on their list of priorities." She swallowed. "The process is fresh in my mind. Perhaps, when this is over, I'll put pen to paper." *Perhaps.*

She brushed aside a stray tear. Decision reached, she tossed the folded sheets of paper onto the smoldering coals, and watched as their edges sparked, caught fire, and disintegrated into ash.

CHAPTER TWELVE

White-faced but resolute, Aileen climbed into the steam wagon beside her grandfather. The vehicle chuffed and puffed as pistons churned inside their cylinders, ready to propel them down the rutted road. William held the steering pole, his face bright with excitement, no doubt relishing the potential for danger, for a sword fight, for a new life in the city.

"Do not," Natalia warned for what must be the twenty-third time, "under any circumstances, skirmish with Ivanov or Kravchuk. Keep your charges well in mind. You must reach Edinburgh *safely.*"

"I've already given you my word." William pulled his wiry shoulders back and puffed out his narrow chest. "Repeatedly. We'll reach your Edinburgh townhouse. The Russians have no interest in me, and," he glanced at

Aileen, "nothing but disdain for that which they ought to value." He squinted at the horizon where the bright sun crept into a cloudless sky. A rare, spring event in Scotland. "Best take advantage of the light."

Pteryformes were, by nature, nocturnal. Not that they couldn't be roused and coaxed—with the promise of fresh meat—to fly during daylight. A highly likely and unfortunate possibility. With a final nod and a sharp tug at the steering pole, William set the steam wagon in motion.

"We need to hurry." Luke caught at her hand, yanking her thoughts back to their most-pressing situation.

Together they dashed back through the castle's gate—locking it behind them—and into the kitchens where Zia paced, unsettled, beside the brazier and her three eggs, well aware that today's activities were anything but routine. Her tongue flicked as she rushed toward them with unusual speed and reared back to drop her clawed front feet on Luke's thighs.

"It's okay." He stroked a hand over her head. "You'll love the mountains, the rocks. So much more interesting than a boring castle. A new home. A new friend." He grinned. "With luck and a handful of years, perhaps grand-dragonets."

Natalia snorted. It was a few hours travel up the River Teith to Callander, their gateway into the highlands and, from there, the Trossachs. Not that either of them expected to reach it before their hasty departure was discovered. Odds were trouble would arrive long before they reached the small village.

She lifted the heavy coal scuttle—lined as it was with river stones heated for the first leg of their journey—that held Zia's clutch and turned toward the stairway that led downward to the postern door in the curtain wall. Slinging their rucksack across his shoulder, Luke hefted the brazier and its carefully banked fire and followed.

A quick turn of the iron key in the door, and they stepped outside the relative safety of the castle's walls and struck out upon the path that led to the river's edge. Low-hanging branches caught at her hair, at the braid she'd carefully plaited and re-pinned about the crown of her head. Though she hurried, she was careful not to trip upon rocks and roots that jutted from the uneven ground at her feet. Dropping her precious cargo was not an option.

A few minutes later she stopped at the river's edge, searching for the boat Luke swore he'd examined last night while she slept. He slipped past and began tossing aside a layer of cut branches and underbrush to reveal their escape vessel: a small dinghy—its wood so old and rough they were certain to end with splinters. An odd—and equally old—motor was bolted to its stern. Everything would fit, but without much room to spare. He tossed their rucksack into the boat, beside a reassuring cache of assorted weapons, then shoved the boat halfway into the shallow water that rushed past.

Holding her hand, Luke steadied her while she stepped into the boat as it wobbled on its keel. *It would be fine*, her mind insisted, once they were out on the water. Providing it didn't leak. Or the motor didn't seize.

Luke caught her curious glance. "A modified Trouvé outboard. A bit rusty, but I was able to coax it back to life." He lifted Zia into the dinghy, then very carefully placed the brazier and the coal scuttle into the hull. "Hang on."

He gave the boat a great shove, and then leapt onto it as the current caught it, turning the vessel downstream toward Stirling. *Away* from the Trossachs. Natalia caught up the oars, straightening them, doing what she could to keep them from drifting too far while Luke cranked the flywheel. A moment later, the engine roared to life, and he dropped onto a seat, gripped the tiller, and steered them upstream. She tucked away the oars and turned her attention to their weapons cache.

Clipping her quiver to her belt, she caught up her crossbow. When they were discovered—for it was inevitable, especially given the din of the outboard motor—arrows would be their first and best line of defense. She notched one in place, careful to avoid its metal-tipped point as she cranked the tension spring.

Only then did she look up. The rising sun illuminated the flowing river with a brilliant, golden light. A beautiful dawn in a cloudless sky. Excellent for spotting an approaching enemy.

Still, despite her intended vigilance, Natalia's gaze drifted downward to Luke. His thick, dark hair blew in the wind, while the rising sun threw the planes of his face into both light and shadow. She marveled at the ripple of muscle beneath fabric. At the complete and total restoration of his strength.

His eyes danced when he caught hers, and he grinned. Desire sparked inside of her as she returned his smile. There was no denying the exhilaration that accompanied an infusion of dragon stem cells. She'd certainly enjoyed the sexual potency they'd bestowed upon him.

A screech tore through the air, and a dark silhouette appeared in the sky. Pteryformes. Zia opened her mouth, echoing the call with her own primal cry before draping herself over the scuttle that held her clutch, wings outstretched.

Dammit, she'd hoped for more time. Ivanov and Dimitri must have set a watch to have discovered William's departure so quickly, to have questioned him, to have already redirected their attention back to Castle Kinlarig and its surrounds.

Tempting as it was to turn toward the shore in anticipation of a fight, open water was their best hope of gaining an advantage; when the pteryformes swooped toward them, she could take better aim without trees to block her sight. Luke's shoulders tensed. Wrapping rope about the tiller, he lashed the outboard motor in place and pointed the boat directly up the river, buying them a few minutes of hands-free navigation before they reached the first bend.

He dragged forth a long rifle and proceeded to breech-load a bullet into the weapon.

Her jaw dropped. "How did you find bullets?" she called. She'd hunted throughout the castle, hoping to find a stash. Even offering a silver tea set to the townspeople in trade for a handful of bullets. But they were nowhere to be found.

"In the pockets of Rathail's hunter," he called back over the noise of the engine.

Of course. She should have thought to look.

Regardless, the crossbow was her weapon. Hours upon hours spent in the castle courtyard at target practice. She'd skewered one man, why not a flying reptile?

As the shadow of its great wings passed overhead, she squinted and took aim. "On the right!" she yelled, claiming her mark. Though she had little chance of hitting Dimitri from this angle, nothing would please her more than to drop his ride from underneath him.

Luke too had a score to settle, but he pointed his rifle toward the beast on the left, aiming for Ivanov and leaving Dimitri to her. Pride swelled in her chest. In this fight they were well-matched, each counting on the other's skills to elude capture.

Bullets splashed into the water beside them; the report of gunfire followed.

Thwack. Her arrow flashed through the sky and tore a hole through the Dimitri's mount's leathery wing. She cursed. Not enough damage to slow the flying reptile. There was nothing to do but pray the tip of the arrow had sent enough venom burning through its wing to discourage cooperation with its handler.

Bang. Ivanov screamed as Luke's bullet hit its mark.

Round one fell to them.

Luke reloaded.

She notched another arrow as the pteryformes banked and turned, swooping lower this time. Again, she aimed for the only spot that might prove vulnerable on the oversized, featherless bird: where wing met body.

Bullets slammed into the wood of their boat, shattered slivers erupted into the air. The boat rocked, and Zia bellowed her displeasure at the threat to her clutch.

Thwack. Bang. They both fired at once. A bullet struck Dimitri, but he held fast as his beast circled higher into the sky. The arrow, however, tore through the second creature's forearm, and Ivanov's pteryform screamed, rearing away and crashing into the trees along the bank, ripping its rider from its back. Ivanov fell, striking the riverbank with a thud, his neck bent at an unnatural angle. A dark glee rushed through her at the fitting death of a vile man who had so casually and coldly thought to put a convenient end to Luke's life.

"A brilliantly placed arrow," Luke said, flashing her an approving smile that made her heart swell with pride. "One down."

But there was no time to enjoy their victory; the first bend of the river approached. Luke tossed his rifle aside, then cut the engine. They would not crash headlong into the riverbank, but they now lost the advantage of speed, of controlling—to some degree—their direction. Silence descended as the boat began to drift slowly downstream.

Luke lifted a finely-honed rapier and slid a dagger from his belt. "Only three bullets remained in the dead hunter's pocket." The gold flecks in his eyes glinted.

"Worth hauling that rifle along, however, if only to injure that bastard, Kravchuk."

The final pteryform aloft turned, circling back toward them.

Momentary elation quickly faded and was replaced by renewed fear. The danger was not at all past. "Be careful," she begged. "Dimitri might want to capture me alive, but he won't spare a second thought for your life."

"He needs to be killed," Luke stated flatly. "He can't be allowed to escape, to return to Russia with news of anything, including our location."

"Agreed." With a glance at Zia, at the eggs, Natalia reassured herself of their relative safety, then braced her legs and lifted her crossbow once more. Icy resolve steeled her spine as she prepared to take down her former fiancé before his mount flew close enough that Luke would find a use for his sword.

With a blood-curdling cry, the winged reptile folded its wings, obscuring Dimitri—her would-be target—and dove.

Luke swore and lifted his blade. "Does he mean to sink us?"

"Possibly."

Correcting for speed, distance, drift and wind, Natalia took her best shot. And missed. Before she could reload, a flash of light glinted off silver metal, and Dimitri dropped onto their boat with a crash, blade in hand. "I've come for what is rightfully mine," he snarled.

"I belong to no one save myself," Natalia replied, chin lifted. "And a dragon should never be subjected to your oversight."

"We'll see about that."

The boat rocked violently, scattering hot coals from the brazier as Dimitri stomped over the cache of weapons, intent on slicing Luke's neck. Natalia dropped her crossbow and bent to draw a knife from her boot— one she could throw—all while reaching with her free hand to splash river water into the boat. A hiss of steam rose into the air. Fire averted, she waited, watching for an opening to enter the fray, but Luke and Zia stood between her and the Russian. Heart in her throat, she reached for the coal scuttle, helping Zia to drag the precious eggs away from the fight.

Luke deflected the first attack with relative ease, and shock rippled across Dimitri's face. "What is this?" he asked, brow furrowed. Assured of easy prey by Ivanov's poisoned blade, the Russian had dropped onto their boat unprepared to struggle for a victory. She hoped it was a fatal mistake.

With a roar, Luke attacked.

Blades clanged and slashed through the air, with Luke's newfound strength lending him the upper hand as the boat drifted ever closer to the shore. *Slash!* Blood bloomed on Dimitri's shirt. *Rip!* The Russian retaliated, slicing though the cloth covering Luke's thigh. Blood seeped forth.

The battle raged on.

Zia lunged, sinking her venom-laced teeth into Dimitri's ankle. The Russian yelled, striking out at the beast latched to his boot as Luke took aim at Dimitri's side. The boat rocked, nearly tipping them all into the river.

An opening. But as Natalia adjusted her grip on the hilt of her knife, preparing to throw, a dark shadow swooped low. With a rush of cool air, Dimitri's pteryform stretched out a clawed leg. But not to save its master or to carry away the man battling against him. Instead, it snatched the handle of the coal scuttle, lifting the dragon eggs into the sky.

"No!" But her scream was futile. Somehow that cursed beast had recognized the precious cargo they carried.

With a blood-curdling howl, Zia launched herself from the boat and into the river. *Splash.* Her short legs churned furiously and her small wings flapped as she swam the short distance to the shore in desperate pursuit of her young.

Dread clawed at Natalia's throat. If the beast dropped its plunder, there was no chance the tiny dragonets—still within their leathery shells—would survive. Rage blazed as she narrowed her gaze back upon the man who had—with cold-hearted intent—set in motion the events that brought them to this desperate day.

Rage pounded in her ears, but with the pteryform in the sky, there was nothing to be done. Save end the man who had initiated this attack.

Thud. The dingy bumped, then scraped along the edge of the river. Catching on unseen rocks and debris beneath the water's surface, it began to tip onto its side.

"Go!" Luke yelled.

She leapt from the boat and into mud. Luke vaulted to land beside her. Together they ran up the riverbank, over the rocks and weeds, seeking solid footing.

Dimitri followed.

The sword fight resumed, and the clang of blades rang through the woods as the two men attacked and parried, occasionally grappling in close quarters or drawing blood. Neither managed to land a serious wound, though she could see Dimitri weakening from the dragon venom.

Crouching, blade in hand, Natalia waited. She threw occasional glances at the sky, watching with her heart in her throat, to track where the pteryform might land. It was circling the field just beyond the copse of trees beside them. Should it land, there might still be hope that they could rescue the eggs.

Luke shifted his approach and attacked, forcing Dimitri to dodge sideways and driving him backward. *Toward her.* For a heartbeat, their gazes met. He was offering her the chance to extract her revenge. For her injury, her father's death, her exile. And for hurting the man she loved.

Now.

With ice in her veins she lunged, slicing deeply through the muscles of Dimitri's back. He screamed as blood welled, then stumbled. As he struggled for balance, realization washed over his face. He could no longer hope to fend them both off. Not with dragon venom pumping through his veins. All but dead, yet still on his feet, he *turned his back* on Luke and locked his heated gaze on her.

"Why so much hate? Why couldn't you just let us go?" she yelled. Her muscles shook with emotion, with a need to understand.

"If only you'd had the decency to die when you fell from that cave, I wouldn't have had to spend the last three years living under your father's shadow." A sneer pulled at his lips. "You and your father's foolish altruism held us all back, when so much power easily lay within our grasp. He should have shared the potential of his work. With *me*."

Dimitri charged.

She lifted her blade and stood her ground.

Fffftt! Luke's blade pierced Dimitri's torso—from back to front.

Eyes wide, the Russian staggered, wrapping his hands about the blade that protruded from his chest, as if he might manage to pry it free and resume the fight. But blood welled in his mouth and trickled from its corners. He stumbled. *Snap!* The thin blade broke in two. With a look of shock, he collapsed to the ground.

Natalia stood, shaking. The man who had betrayed her father, who had tortured the man she loved, was dead. A man she'd once thought to marry. Ought she feel something other than the cold pleasure of justice?

~~~

It was over. Luke stared at the dead man lying on the ground waiting to feel something. Relief? Remorse? Elation? All he could summon was disgust. For the wasted opportunities and resources that Kravchuk had thrown away like a child who could never be satisfied, no matter the bounty laid at his feet.

"Zia's eggs!" Natalia yelled, tipping her face upward to search the trees above her. She stepped backward, tripping over Kravchuk's body.

Luke caught her, wrapped his arms about her waist and pressed a quick kiss to her lips. *Aether*, his heart nearly burst with love. She'd fought so bravely. "Eggs?"

Finding her balance, she pointed behind him at the winged creature the Russian had ridden. "When Dimitri dropped onto the boat, the pteryform snatched away the coal scuttle!"

Shit. Not over. His arms loosened their hold even as his muscles tensed, readying themselves for another battle.

"The creature was circling, coming in for a landing nearby, over there in the field. But—" Natalia's hand fell upon his arm. "You seem fine, but you're wounded."

"Mostly superficial cuts. We'll see to them later." He looked over her shoulder, searching through the undergrowth for the missing dragon. "That explains why Zia leapt from the boat."

There was a roar, followed by an ear-piercing shriek. An unmistakable sound of two enraged reptiles.

"Zia!" Natalia cried.

He and Natalia took off at a run. Just beyond the trees, a field opened before them where Zia snarled and gnashed her teeth, facing down a wounded pteryform some five times her size. The pteryform hissed and clawed the ground. Snapping, it lunged. But Zia darted out of reach, turning her head to spit venom onto the beast's broadside. As the toxin frothed and bubbled atop its thick hide, a faint odor of sulfur—as if someone had struck a match—rose into the air.

Zia was holding her own. He bit back his praise, lest he distract her.

With a roar, the pteryform threw its head backward and let loose a furious cry.

"There!" Natalia pointed.

Behind the pteryform, the coal scuttle lay tipped upon its side. One egg was still nestled midst the warm stones. Two others had rolled free, their gold streaks glimmering in the sunlight.

She grabbed at his hand, yanking him along as she crouched low to run behind the distracted pteryform, all but diving headlong into the undergrowth. Together, they half-walked, half-crawled along the edge of the field, skulking past the dueling creatures until they were only a few yards away from the dragon eggs.

Without warning, Natalia dashed out from their sketchy cover and snatched up the handle of the coal scuttle, pulling it back into relative safety. One egg saved. But pteryformes had excellent hearing, and it turned on its hind legs with a roar, searching the underbrush to find another foe at its back. Stretching its neck, the creature took a step forward.

Luke dragged Natalia behind the thick trunk of a tree. Staying was foolish—they ought to turn tail and run—but leaving the two eggs, leaving Zia to fend for herself wasn't an option.

Zia let loose an enraged squeal, then flutter-hopped behind the pteryform, snapping and biting at its ankles. Venom dripped from Zia's jaws as her teeth sank into the tough hide, and the rotten smell of hydrogen sulfide grew stronger.

Distracted, the pteryform turned again to hiss at this not-insignificant annoyance.

Though bloody and battered, energy still coursed through Luke's veins. He credited the stem cells. Crouching low, he braced his feet against the ground and prepared to run. "I'll grab the eggs. Can you cover me?"

Pushing the coal scuttle behind the trunk of a tree, Natalia drew a throwing knife from her boot. She tested the weight of the blade in her hand. "There's little chance I can do more than cause it a moment's annoyance."

He pointed at a farmhouse in the distance; they needed walls if they were to stand a chance against the pteryform's sharp beak and massive claws. "Then we run. We reach its door, then draw the creature's attention, give Zia a chance to find cover."

She nodded. "Ready?"

"Ready." He tensed.

Natalia stepped into the open and took a deep breath, focusing on her target. Waiting. She gave a sharp whistle and the great winged reptile turned, surveilling her with a single enormous eye. As the blade left her hand, Luke darted forward, gathering up a dragon egg in each arm, tucking them close to his chest before veering into the thin cover of the underbrush toward the coal scuttle.

From the corner of his eye, he saw the enormous creature rear back, a knife embedded in the side of its torso just beneath the front edge of its wing. Zia darted forward, ripping a chunk of flesh from the beast's hindquarters.

Skidding through forest detritus to the coal scuttle, Luke dropped the two eggs inside and closed his hand about the handle, every muscle tensed for escape.

"Wait," Natalia said, pointing.

Above the field, a shadow passed. He looked up with dread. The other pteryform had returned and now circled, calling to its companion below. The grounded—and wounded—creature replied with a ground-shaking roar, then began to flap its enormous wings, rising into the air.

At his side, Natalia called to Zia, urging the dragon into the copse of trees at the river's edge, all while taking steps in the direction of the farmhouse. Should the two pteryformes decide to attack, amidst the tree trunks, they would find it difficult—though not impossible—to maneuver.

But though the cries of the two beasts rent the air and shattered the morning peace for miles, they no longer had masters to command them and their forms circled ever higher into the sky. Perhaps, seeing no reason to continue to tangle with sharp and biting adversaries without good reason, they sought a lair to lick their wounds and hide from the bright morning sun. Not that Luke cared. Their silhouettes disappeared into the distance.

The dragon bumped against his leg, tipping her head sideways to inspect the contents of the scuttle he held. He set it upon the ground and ran a hand over her head. "There you go, Zia. Safe and sound."

He turned and Natalia threw herself into his arms, wrapping hers about his neck, triumph flashing in her eyes. "We did it!"

He pulled her against his chest. "Accomplished the impossible at least three times since dawn." Desire flared, and he spun her around, pressing her back to the bark of the tree, spreading his fingers wide to grip the flare of her hips.

Her eyes darkened. "Only a kiss." Her voice was husky. "We're about to have company."

In the distance, William's voice called. With only a few minutes until they were discovered, Luke reined in every instinct. Save one. Dragons. A sword fight. And the battle won. Claiming the lips of a lady—his love— felt as necessary as drawing his next breath.

EPILOGUE

Natalia stood beside Luke atop a rocky promontory overlooking Loch Lubnaig as Zia and Sasha acquainted themselves with each other. Over rough grasses and scattered scree, they walked side by side, tongues flicking as they explored the many cracks and crevices, searching for a space to serve as a home.

"Took you long enough," Luke's brother said, then muttered under his breath about fire-spitting dragons and sparks and the inconvenience of an entire wardrobe of now-charred clothing. Michael Dryden—waiting impatiently for over a week in the Trossachs—had happily turned over care of the young male dragon to them. He slapped his brother on the shoulder. "Looks like Scotland agrees with you."

Luke snorted, but didn't elaborate.

With little more than a sideways glance and a twist of his lips, he'd taken in Luke's restored health and dropped the keys to a small cottage—where the dragon eggs rested, warm and safe beside the hearth—into his hands. Soon, their tiny egg teeth would pierce through the shells and they would have their hands full. "I'm needed back at the estate. Send a skeet pigeon when you pick a date." With a grin, he departed.

William had caught the empty, flat-bottomed boat as it drifted past them on the road to Stirling, then turned back for Castle Kinlarig to look for its missing occupants. Relieved to find them safe, if bruised and battered, he'd happily reported that Aileen and McKay were unharmed. After discovering the bed of the wagon held not much but crated swords and armor, the Russians had spotted the ploy and wasted little time with questions before taking to the air.

Adjourning briefly to the castle for bandages and fresh supplies, Natalia had given William a fierce hug and promised to visit the city soon. Then she and Luke had set out once again upon the River Teith, reaching the small town of Callandar—unmolested—by late afternoon. Inquiries directed them to his brother, some distance further north alongside Loch Lubnaig. Unwilling and unable to stop, lest they reveal the reality of dragons, they pressed onward. Sleeping—for the most part—beneath the stars, they'd reached his brother's temporary residence the following day.

Alone at last, Luke cleared his throat. "I retract my earlier suggestion. That you marry a wealthy gentleman. Let the castle crumble. So long as we're together—"

"I refuse to be your kept woman." His gaze snapped to hers, but she softened her harsh words with flashing eyes and laughter that rose to ride upon the wind. "I insist we marry." She pressed a palm to her heart. "I love you. I have ever since you first taught me the proper way to wield a sword." Waving a hand, she continued. "I don't wish to own a castle, Luke. I've had enough of its dark, dank stone walls. A distant relative of some consequence wishes to purchase the rock pile and its lands. No doubt keen to style himself the next laird."

He grinned. "Is this a proposal, Lady Kinlarig?"

"It is." She swatted his arm. "Don't be difficult. Will you marry me, Luke Dryden?"

"You wish to live with a dragonkeeper in a cottage beside a loch?" He tipped up her chin.

"For now. Provided we spend a portion of each year in the city so that I might consult with colleagues. We'll need to install a small laboratory, of course. And eventually, we'll need more room for the children."

"Children?" His eyes lit up.

"Several." Leaning into his touch, she lifted her hands to his shoulders, drawing him closer still. Brushing her lips over his. "Say yes."

"Yes," he whispered, then nipped her earlobe sending a tremor of need through her entire body.

Her next words came on a gasp. "The cottage bed looked sturdy. Shall we investigate?"

"Immediately." He scooped her into his arms and strode down the hillside.

Laughing, she wrapped her arms about his neck, planning all the different ways they might make use of a—relatively—empty cottage.

~~~~~

84229244R00129

Made in the USA
San Bernardino, CA
06 August 2018